Finding Teo

This is an IndieMosh book

brought to you by MoshPit Publishing
an imprint of Mosher's Business Support Pty Ltd

PO Box 4363
Penrith NSW 2750

indiemosh.com.au

Copyright © Marjorie Morrissey 2021

The moral right of the author has been asserted in accordance with the Copyright Amendment (Moral Rights) Act 2000.

All rights reserved. Except as permitted under the Australian Copyright Act 1968 (for example, fair dealing for the purposes of study, research, criticism or review) no part of this publication may be reproduced, stored in a retrieval system, or transmitted in any form or by any means, electronic, mechanical, photocopying, recording or otherwise, without the written permission of the publisher.

A catalogue record for this work is available from the National Library of Australia

https://www.nla.gov.au/collections

Title: Finding Teo

Author: Morrissey, Marjorie (1955–)

ISBNs: 9781922703279 (paperback)
9781922703286 (ebook – epub)
9781922703293 (ebook – Kindle)

Subjects: FICTION/Literary; World Literature Australia; Women; Cultural Heritage

This story is entirely a work of fiction. No character in this story is taken from real life. Any resemblance to any person or persons living or dead is accidental and unintentional. The author, their agents and publishers cannot be held responsible for any claim otherwise and take no responsibility for any such coincidence.

Cover concept by Marjorie Morrissey.

Cover design and layout by Robin Hall.

Cover image adapted from "Corfu Island Greece" by massonth and licensed under CC BY-NC-SA 2.0

Finding Teo

Marjorie Morrissey

For Robin and Jack

Anna

My family doesn't do parties by halves. Getting together to celebrate only one event isn't complex enough. Tonight's no different. It's my bon voyage. It's a welcome for a distant relative I've yet to meet as an adult. It's my grandparents' wedding anniversary. It's real Australian Easter. It's close enough to St Patrick's Day for a late drink or two. It's soon-to-be Greek Easter. It's also the day of the early Irish Easter Uprising and a few days after Greek Independence Day. I don't think we're doing May Day tonight.

I'm running late, even for Greek dinnertime. Mum will be in 'organising-Jo' mode and will not be happy. The old people will all be there. Having a party the night before I head to Greece was not my idea. But I only get one vote. As Yiayia always reminds me, real democracy is about listening and considering everyone's point of view. Daddo always says that, as the Greeks invented democracy, we should go along with her thinking. Obviously, a flight at seven o'clock in the morning did not sway family democracy on this occasion.

I'm the first customer my Uber driver's ever driven. From Sudan, she arrives on time, drives calmly through the drizzling rain and is delighted to be taking me to a family gathering. The strains of 'Zorba the Greek' float towards us as we pull up to the Community Club. The septuagenarian band must be playing. They mostly do funerals these days but are up for anything.

Definitely waving not drowning. As I farewell my driver, the music switches to 'Galway Bay', played with a bouzouki.

I follow the sound of the music and the smell of the food through the foyer, across the blue and green shag pile carpet to the rear of the building, where balloons have been placed at the door of the self-catering function room, heralding the private event. In the distance, I see Mum, who casts me a look that says, 'You're late (again)'. She's already been cornered by Father Padraig.

There's no time to scan the room before Yiayia's arms suck me into its centre. 'Anna, come and meet Theo,' she says. 'You two were babies together.' I hate the way old people get pleasure out of throwing together two adults who last saw each other when they were wearing nappies, but this could be a bit different. He's hot. Theo and I air kiss. Over his shoulder, I see Yiayia's chorus of catering commandos, a team of short, round, black-clad women, stream from the small kitchen with platters of dips, olives, casseroles, lamb, roasted vegetables, stuffed tomatoes, spanakopita and sausages.

'No austerity here, eh?' Theo asks.

'None,' I reply. 'Yiayia's friends will have all brought something. It's not a competition, of course, except that it is.' He smiles. We stand together a bit awkwardly as the platters flow out from the kitchen, giving no hint that technically we should still be fasting, as it's not quite Australian Easter or Greek Easter.

'At my farewell in Athens, my friends and I ate souvlaki from our favourite hole-in-the-wall near Syntagma Square as a demonstration took place behind us,' Theo tells me. I really want to hear more but my opportunity is cut short. Mum gives me the quickest and curtest of hellos under the fluorescent lights and then steers Theo away, squeezing him between Yiayia and Daddo, at the head of the long banquet table, decorated with blue-and-white paper tablecloths. *Bugger.* She quickly returns and plonks me beside Father Padraig (*double bugger*) and his Guinness, before heading to the other end of the table, ostensibly to 'be near the kitchen to keep an eye on the food'; as if she stands any chance against the commandos.

Daddo stands, signals to the band to stop and hollers, 'Peia and I wish you all a hundred thousand welcomes. Chefs, a hundred thousand thanks. Guests, a hundred thousand blessings.' With that, the band transitions into the dinner music and the guests understand that tonight, juxtapositions of 'Galway Bay' and 'Zorba the Greek' will be perfectly normal.

The second leg of the food relay starts. Mounds of dolmades, served by their makers, arrive. Kolokithokeftedes follow closely behind them before a seamless baton change occurs and the tiropitakia appears. In the midst of the Food Olympics, Father Padraig rattles endlessly on about the 1916 Easter Uprising and its looming centenary next year.

Padraig is a friend of Daddo. Actually, he was a friend of Daddo's mother, my great grandmother, Josephine, whom I never met. Mum says Padraig is the most modest part of Daddo's modest inheritance and that Yiayia only tolerates him because he's a good friend to Daddo. They spend many happy hours together on the craic, having a good wallow in their Irishness. Padraig's younger than Daddo but older in his thinking. Mum says he somehow missed Vatican Two. Tonight, he's in his full central-casting fifties Irish priest garb. It's a serious look. Black suit. Round white collar. Big ears. Shiny head.

The members of Yiayia's commando chorus keep wary eyes on each other. I swear they are all wearing the same mask. One tempts me with dolmades, urging me to find, 'A Nice Greek Boy while I'm away'. Then a potential Gold Medal winner segues in, suggesting that finding 'A Nice Greek Boy' at my 'advanced age' is surely more important than this 'career thing that I'm about to do'. All the while, A Nice (?) Hot Greek Boy sits crushed between my grandparents.

For a moment, I think of engaging in some Socratic questioning with members of the chorus by asking questions like, 'How would you verify or disprove your assumption about "A Nice Greek Boy"?' or 'What might be an alternative to a "Nice Greek Boy"?'. However, after catching Mum's eye, I decide to simply extol the virtues of their food with which I fill my mouth.

Jo

The dagger look Anna throws my way tells me that she's not at all happy with my choice of her dinner companion. I decided to give her the gift of sitting next to Father Padraig for being late (she's always late). From my end of the table, I see Theo is chatting with Mama. I know that he'll also be receiving dollops of gratuitous advice with each bite of food. Mama's friend, Calandra Chaconas, taps me on the shoulder.

'Just look at her,' she says. 'She loves the young generation and is great on advice for them. That young man will be eating her wisdom.'

'Yes,' I answer. 'She is a living, breathing confessional. Anna tells her more than she tells me. I don't know what it is, but young people tell her their most personal stories. She has the oracle thing.'

Calandra laughs, nodding her head in agreement. 'It happens everywhere. In these settings and out in the world. When young tradies fix things for her at home, they tell her everything. And I mean *everything*.' She certainly hears more about the detail of others' lives than they hear about hers. Calandra continues, 'And look at your lovely Anna. I will go and give her a big farewell hug now before the night gets too busy.'

I hate these fused multi-celebration nights at which I am always stuck right in the middle of Mama's determination, Da's toleration and Anna's capitulation. Mama always says she will do all the work required and, back in the day, she did. However, at eighty-one years old, it's now all a bit too much for her, so she expects me to do the work. She has her 'friends' to help but, with the exception of Calandra, they require constant oversight. They would be a full-time job for the United Nations. Looking after Mama and Da is getting harder. They think they live independently; a hell of a lot of time and effort goes into sustaining that myth.

I can see Padraig is in early oratorical flight and a sudden pang of maternal guilt propels me in Anna's direction. As I approach, I hear Padraig: 'And those ANZAC soldiers were brainwashed into shooting their kith and kin in the Easter Uprising.' He is actually a pacifist, but you have to live through a lot of bloody battles to gain that knowledge. He eats another mouthful. It is usually around this time that he draws breath and begins to quote Einstein. I catch a look of determination and desperation in Anna's eyes as he says, 'Einstein claimed nothing would end war unless the people themselves refused to go to war.'

She tilts her head to the left side, flicks her hair from her right shoulder and propels her intense and, tonight, sparkling eyes at me. 'Mum, isn't it lovely that I get to spend my last night in Australia with Father Padraig here?' Her sarcasm oozes through her painted lips. 'I was just telling him of my youth theatre performance in Lysistrata: such a great anti-war play.'

I am quite glad that I missed that part of their conversation, but I am now feeling more than a bit guilty about setting up this seating arrangement. However, I also know that Anna would have relished telling Padraig that the Greek women withheld sex from their husbands until both sides agreed on peace terms. 'Anna, can you help me with something?' I ask.

She jumps at the out I have just provided. 'Of course, Mum.' It is wet as Anna and I sit outside under the awning. 'I don't deserve Father Padraig tonight,' she says as she lights a cigarette and offers me one.

I look longingly at her offering. 'I was just trying to get the food moving along so you can get some pre-flight sleep,' I reply. The packet remains open before me. 'Anna, it's been nearly a year. I don't want to test my resolve.'

'Oh, come on,' she says. 'We won't get to do this again for a while. Just one?' The details of the lectures I have given her over the years about resisting peer pressure vanish. I love having a cigarette with her. We each drop our resolve for the time being. I light up and sigh. My shoulders drop and my neck unwinds. It is a pity it feels so good. She continues, 'The food could have happened if I had sat with Yiayia, Daddo and Theo. He's just a bit better looking than Padraig and I'd like to know why he's back just as I'm about to leave Australia.'

'*Sygnómi*,' I say. 'Sorry.' I pause and think about telling her how much I'm going to miss her, but my need to keep the show on the road kicks in. Instead I ask, 'Are you still okay to do the anniversary toast?' She nods. 'Mama wants to toast your bon voyage so that leaves me with St Patrick's Day, early Easter Uprising and early Greek Independence Day.'

She sighs as she looks at me and adds, 'Just don't let Padraig near the Easter Uprising on this Blood Moon Easter Saturday.' We manage a laugh as the rain splashes near us and we sit quietly finishing our cigarettes. The butts go in her portable ashtray: a fresh mint tin. We can be like flint and rock, but I am not sure how I will keep it all together when she's gone. We each take a mint from her real fresh mint tin and return inside. Even the rain on the roof is not loud enough to quell the infectious noise of the celebration crowd.

I catch Mama's eye. She looks like a stunning and ageless oracle tonight. She could easily be Olivia Dukakis's twin sister. I could be Dawn French's twin sister. Mama flashes her eyes at someone who flashes her eyes to someone else who then begins to clear the plates from the table. Anna and I head up to Mama and Da. He too looks wonderful and just like Jimmy Carter. Tonight, his Irish eyes are in full twinkle, shining steadfastly out from under his full head of auburn hair. We sit down. Theo and Anna both smile. They seem happy to be in each other's company. Maybe I've finally done something right tonight. Da gives his eye to the band, which strikes up once again. The chief crooner commences:

If you ever go across the sea to Ireland,
Then maybe at the closing of your day,

You can sit and watch the moon rise over Claddagh,
And see the sun go down on Galway Bay.

Da already has tears in his eyes as he and his friends join in the singing.

Oh the strangers came and tried to teach us their ways,
And they scorned us just for being what we are,

But they might as well go chasing after moon beams,
Or light a penny candle from a star.

Mama catches my eye. I stand to get things moving along so that we can capitalise on the mood and the tears. I raise my glass and bellow, 'Here's to St Patrick, who's recognised as a good guy by both the Catholic and Greek Orthodox Churches.' Cries of 'Yamas' and 'Sláinte' fill the room, as we drain our glasses a little more. I add, 'And the very good news about this very good guy is that by including him in our celebrations tonight, we are free of fasting.' The crowd goes off and even Mama's team of workers break into bleak smiles. I continue, 'My dear da has a theory—yes, it is a little untested historically and theologically—but according to his theory, St Patrick was behind the 1916 Easter Uprising, which was behind Ireland's ultimate independence. Have some craic with him some time if you want to hear the details. In the meantime, to independence!'

Our glasses are drained a little more. I'm feeling hopeful that we will now move on quickly but then, out of the corner of my eye, I see Padraig grab the microphone off the crooner. I wait, afraid that we might be in for a blast on the Easter Uprising, but what comes forth is the most beautiful voice.

And if there's going be a life hereafter,
And for sure I'm sure that there is going to be,

I will ask my God to let me make my Heaven,
In that dear land across the Irish sea.

One to the Irish. The pacifist priest has nailed it. As the room remains still and quiet, I am ready to approach Greek Independence Day, but I do not even get a chance to navigate around the national holiday celebrating war, before a seventy-something Melina Mercouri look-alike takes the microphone from Padraig, winks at the bandleader and the music slowly begins again. The bouzouki player looks at Mama, inviting her and Da to head to the dance floor. They do so, pulling Theo and Anna along with them.

A line of people forms, facing the room, their arms stretched across each other's arms and their hands resting on each other's shoulders. They pause as Melina Mercouri (actually Calandra) slowly begins to sing.

Oh, you can kiss me on a Monday,
A Monday, a Monday is very, very good.

Or you can kiss me on a Tuesday,
A Tuesday, a Tuesday, in fact I wish you would.

Or you can kiss me on a Wednesday,

A Thursday, a Friday and Saturday is best.

But never, never on a Sunday, a Sunday, a Sunday,
'Cause that's my day of rest.

She has nailed a female kind of Greek Independence Day

without me ever having to say a word. I move to join the dancing line as others do. We sway gently together, smiling to the sound of the bouzouki and the strains of that husky, sexy voice.

Peia

My friend Calandra loves to sing. I love to dance. It's one of the earliest memories I have of being in my mountains in the north of Greece. I think therefore I dance. Dance freezes time. I know I'm at my Community Club in Australia, but I'm really in Greece. A young girl. In our valley. My parents are in the circle. My brother too. As well as people from other families.

Oh, you can kiss me on a Monday,
A Monday, a Monday is very, very good.

Those circles of dancers included everyone. Friends and enemies alike. Dance heals. My mama always said that everything is forgotten once your hands touch the shoulders of the dancer next to you. You trust each other in dance. You forget the recent haggling over the price of a sheep or the feud about whether your small property begins or ends at the tree by the stream. Dance affects the soul. Plato was on to something there.

Or you can kiss me on a Tuesday,
A Tuesday, a Tuesday, in fact I wish you would.

I feel young again. My legs don't ache. My joints are all freed up. My fingers aren't puffy. My knees aren't acting independently. My lower back wants to be part of my upper back. My mind doesn't forget.

Or you can kiss me on a Wednesday,
A Thursday, a Friday and Saturday is best.

Dance does its job in the now. And what a now. All my Australian family are with me. Even Jo is linked in the line. And Theo. Still others continue to join us. One, two, three at a time. Young and old. It's a crazy time in Greece now, but here, tonight, the dance goes on like it did in ancient times.

But never, never on a Sunday, a Sunday, a Sunday,
'Cause that's my day of rest.

Divine dance lives on. Thousands of years of dance. Dance melds. The ancient Greeks fused religion and everyday life and tragedy and comedy.

Anna is leaving us. She says she's taking a chance. Making a choice. I took a chance all those years ago, but it was no choice. However, Anna's confident and ambitious and curious about the world. Piecing it together. I'll miss her so much. Even her just helping me with my phone or sending me funny texts and her always turning up for events like this, time and again. Often by herself. She doesn't seem to need someone constantly by her side. She says she was stuck at her newspaper. That there's more to life. Knowing that, I paid for her airfare. It's our secret. As soon as she submitted her resignation, they offered her more money. But she's still going.

Dance and music unite. Our band is about a thousand years old. The lived life of our singers and players is immense. We dance at religious festivals. We dance at name days. We dance for fertility. We dance during war and during peace. Even Padraig has become Greek for this dance. I see him making for a pile of spare blue-and-white tablecloths. We continue moving in the ever-widening circle as he shakes some open and starts rolling them up like long snakes.

He passes them around and people weave them over their shoulders.

Most of the room has joined the dance. There's no leader. We move with each other, never wanting it to end. That's the reason we're happy to move slowly. We sometimes dance so slowly that we barely move. Deliberately slowly.

But never, never on a Sunday, a Sunday, a Sunday,
'Cause that's my day of rest.

Anna needs her independence, but I don't want to say farewell to her tonight. It's an end and I've never been good at endings.

Anna

As the dance finishes there is silence. Proper silence. No clatter of plates. No chatter. No rain on the roof. I seize the moment and call out, 'Let's take a little break to celebrate Yiayia and Daddo. Sit down. Grab a drink.'

Chairs are dragged. Glasses are filled. Drinks swish. The music starts as four commandos carry in a stretcher-shaped tray, one of them bearing each corner. It's the first time I've heard the 'Chariots of Fire' theme song played on a bouzouki. It's beautiful.

A high cake sits on a tray. It's a traditional blue-and-white Greek Church, sitting atop a green hill, surrounded by the greenest of green fields. A white bell tower rises above the round blue dome of the church and the field is scattered with some fluffy, horned Irish sheep, except the faces of these sheep are blue rather than black. An aesthetic decision, I suppose.

Like in any Olympic ceremony, the cake procession has its moment of drama. The stretcher doesn't exactly glide onto the banquet table. The bell tower wobbles in time with the cross on the top of the church and one sheep takes a dive into Daddo's lap. Time freezes as some stray forks are pulled out from under the stretcher to level the surface of the table. The cake reflects their marriage. Yiayia is the wobbler and Daddo looks after the stray sheep while Mum and I strive to keep the surface level. But I'm not going there tonight. It's up to me to light the Olympic Oratory Flame.

I take a deep breath and begin, 'Yiayia and Daddo. You're here, you're celebrating, you're full of life and you're central to my, so far, short life story.' That bit is true. 'Your love of stories has influenced my love of stories and will influence my journey, which starts tomorrow.' Tick for that too. 'Not many children at primary school knew how to spell "odyssey" or what one was. I did. Same with "banshee".' That's a fact. I used to get weird looks from some of the other kids and I once heard one teacher say to another that I was 'precocious' and liked to 'show off with my words'. 'I'm off on an odyssey. One that each of you has encouraged. I'm a bit scared. And I'm very sad to be leaving you both for a while.' That was also true, but while I am sad to be leaving them, I just have to go. I will go mad if I stay in this family cocoon. It is time to pupate.

'However, you've told me that lots of the world's most interesting people wander at some stage. Like Odysseus, who wandered but always had a home, Ithaca, in his heart.' I really don't count myself as one of the world's most interesting people, but I sure want to meet some of them.

'Yiayia you've said to me, time and time again, "Keep Ithaca always in your mind. Arriving there is what you're destined for. But don't hurry the journey at all".'

I don't know where my home is or where my destiny lies. Bloody Ithaca. Bloody Odysseus.

Took a decade-long gap year after the Trojan War. I continue. '"Better if it lasts for years, so you're old by the time you reach the island, wealthy with all you've gained on the way, not expecting Ithaca to make you rich"'

Theo is looking at me quizzically. One dark eyebrow rises and falls like a bullshit meter. I don't want to take years to make my name. Nor to be poor and old.

'Yiayia and Daddo, Peia and Harry, Happy Sixtieth Anniversary!'

Jo

As well as giving the toast, Anna was meant to get Mama and Da to cut the cake, which uncut looks as though it may be crushed in an assault of happiness. I will need to cordon it off. As I move to the table, I see that Mama's friends are firewalling the cake. The night is getting louder and later. The band is back, playing 'Chariots of Fire'.

A line has formed before Mama and Da. It's almost like people are queuing to meet royalty. They stand in line. They smile. They are patient. Each greeting takes time. Mama in particular treats everyone as though they are the most important person in the room. She is an Olympic Gold Medallist for everyone but me. Breaking in between the over-enthusiastic huggers, I suggest to Mama that it might be a good time to cut the cake, toast Anna and throw in the toasts to the Easters. '*Sigà, sigà,*' she says. Slowly, slowly. That sums us up really. She calls the time. It's Mama's time zone. Never mine.

'Mama, Anna needs to catch a plane in the morning,' I say.

'Jo Jo, Anna is young and now is now. Don't hurry her.'

Anna is talking to Theo. Padraig puts himself in the middle of them and Anna has lost her chance to interview Theo. She catches my eye and I point outside. We both head that way. This time, our cigarettes are lit without any pretence of persuasion or resistance. 'Nice careful speech,' I say.

She ignores my comment. 'Does Padraig have any emotional

intelligence?' she asks rhetorically, inhaling deeply. 'I just want to talk to Theo before I go.'

'You'll never get to go if they don't cut the cake,' I say. I hadn't meant to say that. I didn't need to go there. Not right now.

'Shit. I was meant to cover that in my speech, wasn't I? Sorry, I got distracted.' She is apologising to me. No need for her to do that again tonight. Breathe slowly. Inhale the nicotine. 'So how were Theo and I babies together?' she asks.

'Well, technically, he is Theío Angel's wife's—Theía Beth's—great, grand-nephew. I think. Beth's niece's daughter's son. I knew his mother, Hermioni, who came here sometime when I was in high school. You and Theo were born within months of each other so we all spent a fair bit of time together.'

'Why did they go back to Greece?'

'Hermioni got very homesick after she had Theo and as he was the only grandchild she wanted to be with her mother, who had had a very hard life and was by herself. And, I think Theo's father's father died soon after they returned home and they inherited some land somewhere. So, they went back for a visit and ended up staying there.'

'Why has Theo come back now?' 'I don't know,' I reply. 'Ask him.'

'No luck so far. My mother and a mad Irish priest have been conspiring against me all night.' We pause and admire the roof-gutter waterfall. I decide to say it. 'I am going to miss you.' Her response is too quick. 'Why? Am I the only one who apologises to you?'

That is a bit close for tonight. 'You are the only one who offers me cigarettes and the only one who has any idea about what looking after Mama and Da is like.'

'You'll come and visit me in the summer?'

'That's the plan if I can nail Mama's friends to a care roster.

As you know, they are very hard to pin down.' We finish off our cigarettes and go through the ashtray and breath mint ritual. 'Come on. This cake needs cutting.'

Inside, there is still a hive of huggers around the bride and groom. Mama is in heaven and even Da is loving it. Lapping it up. I catch his eye, point to the cake and mime cutting it. He gives me a thumbs-up, grabs Mama's hand and they head to the cake. From his pocket, he carefully removes the sheep that landed in his lap earlier and places it back among its flock. He then calls for some quiet. He and Mama hold up a blue-white-and-green ribbon-covered knife before plunging it into the field of sheep. Mama takes a deep breath and looks about her. She opens her mouth.

Peia

Breathe. Flutter. Breathe again. I open my mouth waiting for the words. Deep down, I see the letters for 'Anna'. Her name will come out, as long as I keep the two 'n' letters in the middle and the two 'a' letters as the bookends, but they're deep down. Come up to my mouth letters. Come up 'Anna'.

I'll walk towards her. That will make it easier. I'm slow. But I'm old, so nobody expects me to move too quickly. Breathe. Move slowly. Like in the dance. The room is moving in on me.

We just need to move with each other. That's why we're always happy to move slowly. It's sometimes so slow that we barely move. That's what I'm doing.

Anna's letters still aren't coming up to my mouth. I'm quivering in the now. I need a quiver for my letters. I just need to say, 'Anna'. Maybe I have already. The next letters? I need them in my throat. Something is rising in my throat. Could be the letters. Whatever is there is stuck. *Yassou.* Not quite right. You will be missing from me. Letters and words for that? Jumbled. *Tha.* 'You'. *Leípei.* 'Missing'. 'Me'. *Mou.*

I'm missing from me.

My hands just need to touch the shoulders of the dancer next to me. That will warm me up. I feel old. I ache. My joints aren't joined. My letters and words aren't joined. My fingers aren't mine. My knees aren't with me. My lower back isn't part of my upper back. My mind no longer wants to be with my body. My mind isn't in the now. It's going back. I need some shoulders to put my arms around.

There's a young girl. In a mountain amphitheatre. Her brother is there. And her brother's best friend, Adelphos. She's running after Teo and Adelphos. In slow motion. The boys are way ahead. She can usually out-run them both.

Tha mou leípsoun. They will be missing from me.

Anna

Padraig is clearing a space on the floor around Yiayia. 'One. Two. Three. Four.' It's Theo's voice.

Mum is hugging an immobilised Daddo. She looks up and shouts, 'Someone ring 000.' Theo's hands are on Yiayia's chest moving in time to his counting. He's only been here three minutes, but he already knows what to do. I've been here all my life and don't have a clue.

Padraig is talking to Yiayia. 'Peia, can you hear me? Peia, tell me you can hear me.' Theo is counting loudly. 'Twenty. Twenty-one. Twenty-two. Twenty-three.'

Mum screams out, 'They fundraised for a defibrillator here. Someone find the defibrillator.' Mum and her 'someones'. Is this 'someone' meant to be me? A commando breaks ranks from the chorus. She runs like a zeroing missile towards the foyer. Someone be there.

A uniformed person emerges. The manager? She's younger than me, but she's carrying something and is moving quickly. No Greek time now. The manager calls out, 'If you are not doing CPR, move right away. Space, please.' The manager is removing Yiayia's top clothing. Her bra is draped around her neck. She looks so little. So fragile. So old. This must be weird for Theo. He's so close to her. The chorus is turning its combined back on the action. I can hear the quiet clicking of the worry beads. Pads are being attached to Yiayia.

The machine announces, 'Stop CPR. Do not touch patient. Analysing.'

The machine announces, 'Stand clear. Stand clear.' A shock lifts Yiayia like a puppet. The machine continues, 'Commence Compressions.'

Yiayia's pulse. It's not there. Where is it?

The little church looms large. Mum sits Daddo near the uneaten cake and then moves next to Theo and starts counting for him to the beat of the machine's metronome. 'One. Two. Three. Four.' Padraig's hands tenderly cup Yiayia's head. So many times I've watched CPR on television but this is different. I should be doing something. Who called an ambulance? Did that happen?

The manager catches my eye. 'Wait outside,' she calls. 'You, wait outside. Meet the ambulance.'

I have something to do other than nothing. I move to the foyer. In the background I hear, 'Nine. Ten. Eleven. Twelve'. There are people in the foyer. I see Calandra standing by herself. 'I can't be in there,' she says.

'Can you watch for the ambulance?' She nods vigorously and positively, stirred by having something to do. 'Thanks,' I say. She heads outside. I move back to the sea of blue, white and green. She can't leave now. I'm the one meant to be going. Yiayia gets me. Always has. I'm holding back tears. Yiayia would not cry.

I hear Mum's voice. 'Twenty-One. Twenty-Two.'

I tell the manager that Calandra is waiting for the ambulance. She asks me to check Daddo. He could do it. Bring her back for me. I kneel and hold his hands. I move my hands to his shoulders. He puts his hands on my shoulders. My dry eyes briefly meet his wet eyes.

'Thirty.'

Padraig breathes twice into Yiayia's expressionless mouth.

Or you can kiss me on a Wednesday,
A Thursday, a Friday and Saturday is best.

Saturday, now, is so best. Yiayia has to be alive here so I can live over there. 'Daddo. She'll listen to you. Talk to her? Please?' I plead.

'I can't move,' he replies. 'I'll help you.'

He nods. With a slow Daddo, I edge towards Yiayia. I'm doing something. She'll come back. Daddo lowers himself to his knees and speaks to her in his softest lilt. 'Peia. Peia. Hear me.

You're not ready to go to Ithaca yet.' He's crying on his bended knees. He's the softest supplicant next to the quietest oracle. He continues, 'I'm not ready for you to go to Ithaca. Not yet. Please don't hurry there now.'

Jo

Come on, Da, work your magic. Anna is kneeling with Da. There is no twinkle in his Irish eyes now. Just tears. He's begging his wife to come back.

'Nine. Ten. Eleven. Twelve.'

Sigà. Sigà. Slowly. Slowly. We are on Mama's time again. Mama's time zone. Never mine. And here I am stuck in the middle again. I am the counter. The manager is calling the shots. Padraig is doing her breathing. Theo is trying to move her heart. That is what I would like to do. I would love to move her heart. The counting is coming from somewhere within me.

I am with my Móraí Josephine, who hugs me, makes me feel special and understands all my drawings. It is Sunday afternoon. This morning we went to church with Da and saw Father Padraig. After that, we all came back here. Mama is here with friends from her church too. We had a big lunch outside. I sat next to my Móraí. She says that I am the person whom she likes to sit next to the most.

Now, everyone has gone home and we are pottering in her back garden, which is next to Theío Angel's back garden. No fence separates the two gardens. At the end of his garden, near the laneway gate, he works in his long shed, making furniture for the people who come through his door from the laneway under the hanging garlic. He once made me a dark wooden pencil case with a sliding top. On the wall of his shed, there is a fading sketch of a little girl under a cypress tree. That's Mama.

We are planting potatoes, spinach, zucchini, capsicum and eggplant. We hoe the rows. She has her adult hoe and I have my little one made by Theío Angel. I like planting better than weeding. I have left some weeds in the garden near my newly planted seeds. I am distracted by Mórai's nimble hands, which come over mine and grab a towering weed. She tells me that she pulls weeds out before they have time to feel at home and that the best way to make sure that weeding does not feel like a chore is to count out loud as you grab the weeds and throw them away.

'Sixteen,' she calls triumphantly, as she throws one of my big weeds on her pile. 'Your turn now,' she says. 'Grab that next weed and yell out loudly as you toss it on my pile.'

'Seventeen,' I yell.

That is the age I was when Mama told me I had to stop seeing Vasilios. The one boy I really liked. He was Greek for heaven's sake, what other box did he have to tick?

'Eighteen.'

That is the age I was when I was weeding my life big time.

'Nineteen. Twenty.'

I could not catch her eye then. I wish I could catch it now. I have never really looked at her this closely, but I would love her to look at me closely just this once.

'Twenty-Four.'

That is the age I was when I had Anna.

'Thirty.'

That is my daughter's age now. She is about to head off, while here in front of me is Mama, looking like a tiny, helpless baby.

The machine speaks, 'Do not touch patient. Analysing.' 'Stand clear. Stand clear,' the manager calls.

Still no pulse. Come on Mama. Come on. Dance back.

Peia

Burning candles and my wriggling naked baby brother, Teo. The priest blessing the font water. Breathing three times on the oil. Making the sign of the cross three times on Teo's forehead. Cutting a lock of Teo's curly black hair. Dunking Teo in the water three times. My mama is placing him in my arms in a white sheet. Mama borrows him back for a moment. Puts a little white suit on him.

'*Alleluia. Alleluia. Alleluia,*' everyone is singing.

Outside our newly whitewashed church. I'm cradling my little brother. It's busy up here today with his baptism. I often play up here in the church's olive grove, but then it's just me and the sheep and sometimes Vaska and his goats.

My mama is thanking the old women, dressed in black, who whitewashed the church. Some children jump the fence and chase the sheep towards the towering oaks and the shiny acorns that make the polished forest floors. Beyond the oaks, evergreen maples with red-helicopter flares that float to the ground. Further in, chestnuts with their hairy fruit, and gnarled bare-trunked beeches. Then huge plane trees that could house entire families in their nooks and crannies.

I'm allowed to carry Teo home, down our hill, along our path, which is just for feet or hooves. I love being Teo's big sister. I'm smiling. The priest is walking in front of me, like the Pied Piper. He is happy and blessing anything he comes across.

Children. Sheep. Goats. Donkeys. I am concentrating on my precious load, but I can smell the new spring flowers that edge my path and see the different colours on the other paths that weave through our steep valley. So many paths.

Lunches are cooking. Smells of lamb, dill and lemon are wafting up. As they make their way down, people stop off at their homes to collect food for Teo's feast to bring to our home. In winter, when Teo was born, icy winds blew straight through our shutters but now it's spring and we are warm again.

Our place. In our small hallway people come up to me, well, to Teo, and say 'Happy Name Day'. I'm still holding him. I won't let him go. I climb up our narrow stairway, past our bedrooms to the top storey, where our village is gathered in our living room, spilling out onto our balcony and into our courtyard. I can smell our orange trees and the big green cypress tree. Our tree. Our beacon. Visible from all around.

My mama appears and wants to take my bundle of brother. I don't want to surrender him but she convinces me to put him in his crib, in my parents' room. Baby Adelphos is already asleep there. We settle Teo. I tell her that I will look after him.

The other children want to play, but our parents sit us down at our own table in the courtyard. Hunger and plenty take over. We haven't had a feast like this in years. Our little table groans under the weight of hot saganaki cheese, cool tzatziki, bright local greens, smoky sausage, raisin dolmas, lima beans, zucchini flowers and rosemary rabbit.

We finish before the adults sitting at the big table. It is as though they don't want the feasting day to end. We run around outside through the orange trees and play hide-and-seek. Our cypress tree is home base. We squeal as we touch it and once or twice a very little boy, who doesn't understand the rules of this big kids' game, weaves his way through us, waves at us and nearly gives away our hiding place.

I crawl under the big table and hide at Papa's feet. I'm a bit big to fit comfortably but Papa smiles down at me at the same time as he is arguing with the priest. 'We must fight for democracy, we don't need more dictators,' Papa says. I want to ask him more about dictators and democracy, but I know that now is not the time.

At our cypress tree, Agnete, the priest's daughter, has her back to me. She seems to be focused on a shape in the orange grove. It's Vaska but I can't see any goats. I don't want to be caught, so I crawl through a forest of legs and sprint. I don't get caught. I won't be 'it'. I have the home ground advantage.

Several guests start playing instruments. Some are beginning to dance. I want to join in, but first I wander back inside to see if Teo has woken up with all the noise. I head to my parents' room. To Teo's crib. He's not in his crib. Adelphos is still sleeping. Teo has to be in his crib but he's not there. I open my mouth for some words. Nothing comes out. My throat is tight. I want to scream but I freeze. My chest hurts. My head is bursting. I'm sweating. My stomach is in knots. My words are deep down. Come up words. I just need to scream Teo. Something is rising in my throat. Could be the letters. But whatever is there is stuck. *Leípei.* 'Missing'. My words are missing. Teo is missing. I can't move. I need to move. Come on feet.

I sprint into the big room. The music has stopped. There's Mama. No Teo. There's Papa. 'To my son, Teo.' Teo is in his arms. The great big knot is untying. My head is light. My chest is breathing. My heart is bursting. Papa continues, 'This is a significant day. For all of us including this little boy. There are noises in the north that we have resisted so far. We must resist again, for this little boy, for our little girl and for all our children. To all of us here and to those departed. *Yamas.*'

'*Yamas,*' the house echoes.

Jo

The machine announces for the third time, 'Do not touch patient. Analysing.'

Look at me, Mama. Look at me! I have been counting as though my life depends on it. Do it for me, Mama. There is a flutter in Mama's neck. Peia's girls don't cry, but I am close. Da is crying. And here is the cavalry. The paramedics. Slow motion stops. They part us. They talk to Mama. She nods to them. Not to me. But she has danced back. Time is moving again. They are doing what they do. Methodically. Professionally. Soothingly.

I move around to Mama's other side, as one of the paramedics asks me about what happened and when. As I recount the details of Mama's collapse, I see that one side of her face is different to the other. One side is the tragic side of her mask. They tell me that they are doing an electrocardiogram. To check her heart. They are giving her some oxygen. She cannot lift both arms. Only her left arm. When asked her name she calls, 'Teo. Teo.' Theo moves closer to Mama and puts his right hand in her left hand. She takes it and cries.

Mama is back, but she is not all back.

Peia

Papa, with many of the men from our valley, has been in Saloniki a lot during the war. The women are helping each other to grow food. Mama and I have been running our little farm together. Well, she has been doing most of the outside work and I have been doing most of the inside work and looking after Teo and often, Adelphos, while our mothers work outside together.

Teo is asleep upstairs. Mama and I are in our blue kitchen. She is reading an old letter from her Theío Angel in Australia. She hasn't had letters from him since the war started. So, she reads old ones and it makes her happy. I'm doing a sketch of myself standing under our cypress tree. There are some orange trees in the background and behind them is our valley and its winding paths.

Today, Mama has declared a day off. She walks over and examines my sketch. 'That's very good,' she says. 'How about we send it to Theío Angel when we can? He'd love it.'

We are in the garden collecting eggs. I carry them very carefully back into the house. We are making galaktoboureko. She is pouring fresh milk into a saucepan. Our hands are together on the big wooden spoon. We take turns beating the eggs. Then comes the paper-thin pastry. I am allowed to add the melted butter. I layer the pie and she adds the custard. We put it in the hot oven. 'Mama, tell me about Theío Angel.'

'I've told you many times about Theío Angel.'

'Tell me again please. Please.' She smiles. 'Can I sit on your lap?' I'm really too big for her lap but she draws me into her arms, hugs and kisses me and we start my favourite Mama game about her favourite uncle. I start asking the same questions I've asked time and time again. 'Mama, why is Theío Angel your favourite uncle?'

'He is my favourite uncle because he is fun. And when I was little he spoilt me. He didn't have any children of his own.'

'So, Mama, why did he leave?

'He was worried that the King would come back.' I like stories about kings and queens and princes and princesses. I wonder why he was worried that the King would come back. She continues, 'He didn't think the King ruled Greece very well.'

'What's rule?'

'To rule is to boss.'

'Why didn't we need a boss?'

'Well, Theío Angel thought that because the Greeks invented democracy, they could boss themselves better than the King could boss them. He told people that and he also didn't think the King was very fair to everyone.'

'Why did he go so far away?'

'Well, when he was in the last war, he met some Australian soldiers in Saloniki. He liked them and they made him laugh and one of them said that if he wanted to go to Australia he would help him find work. That man helped Theío Angel find his first job there.'

'Were you sad when he went away?'

'I was very sad when he went away, but he promised to write to me and I have lots of his letters from before the war. He spoilt me with his letters. And I have the toys he made for me when I was small.'

She'd never mentioned toys before. 'What toys?' She looks surprised. I haven't asked that before either but I think it is a great way to stretch out our game.

'Well, he made me all sorts of toys. He started with a small carved cypress tree and a sheep to go under it. I loved it. So, he made me more trees. Different sorts. And he carved me donkeys and mountain goats and other animals, like giraffes and elephants and tigers.' She looks dreamy and sighs. She wriggles me off her lap and walks to check the oven. All is well. 'I will just check Teo and be back in a minute.' I inhale the smells escaping from the oven.

She returns. 'Shut your eyes and hold out your hand.' This is another new addition to our game. I stand and scrunch my eyes tight and flatten out my right hand. She places something in it. 'Open your eyes.' It's a beautiful little wooden animal but not one I recognise. It's funny to look at.

I am laughing. 'What is it?'

'It's a kangaroo. Theío Angel sent it to me from Australia. It's actually two kangaroos. That's a baby, called a "joey", in her pouch in the front.' I love it. Happy tears on my cheeks. 'Would you like it? From Theío Angel to me. From me to you. From you to …?' She goes to the oven and carefully lifts out our pie. 'Come on, you can add the sugar syrup to the top.' I do so with my right hand, while my left hand is clutching the kangaroo and its joey.

Anna

It's just after midnight and Theo is giving me a lift in his friend's girlfriend's car. He's charmed someone's vehicle off them, helped to resuscitate Yiayia, held her hand, made her cry and is now driving me to the hospital. 'Are you okay?' he asks.

He's asking about me. 'Yiayia can't do this to me,' I reply. The windscreen wipers are scratching like a cat at a screen door. The downside of the friend's girlfriend's car.

He hesitates a little before asking, 'Do what to you?'

'Be going to hospital in an ambulance after, in all likelihood, suffering a stroke. She knows I need to go to Greece today. It's what Mum says. Yiayia calls the shots on when things happen.' I can't believe I've revealed all that. I'm a journalist. I never blurt things out but just now, I have. I've accused my beloved grandmother—who paid for my airfare—of arranging a stroke to stop me from going to Greece today. The GPS snaps out a direction.

'Need to go or want to go to Greece today?' he queries. He follows the GPS directions and takes the second exit on the left.

'Need and want.' I've done it again. I sound like a cranky kid, not a considered adult.

'So, go,' he says.

I speak slowly and clearly, 'I can't go because Yiayia is in an ambulance going to the hospital. I don't know how bad she is. She might even die.' I'm using my outside voice and it's cracking a little.

Water flows down the windscreen. My tears can't join it. She wouldn't want me to cry. I need her to be okay. I'm tearing up.

'Lots of people recover well from strokes,' he says. He's given me a general answer. I don't believe him, but I like his 'she'll-turn-it-around' scenario.

'I'm not Odysseus. All that Ithaca stuff in my speech about the journey was meant for her, for them, not for me.'

'Yeah, I thought that might have just been in the party spirit. When he was a teenager, my father couldn't wait to get away from Ithaca but he returned there after his father died. Might depend on which bit of your life you're at.'

A set of traffic lights is out. A wet cop in the middle of a big drizzling intersection gestures for us to halt. I'm sobbing now and can't find a tissue in my handbag. 'She can't do this to me now.' There's that little kid again and she's spluttering. 'I've scored a job, all by myself, in Greece, in film, on the other side of the world. I want to go. Today.'

'Do you need a hug?' he asks.

I don't know what I need. The GPS speaks, 'Return to the route'. So accurate. This is not the conversation I had planned to have with Theo. I was going to be journalistic. I was going to be in charge. My questions would have provoked extensive thoughtful answers from him. A kick-start for Greece. I would have been listening to him. Observing him. Yet, here we both are, in a car, facing forward on a wet night. I'm trembling and crying. He's asking the questions and the GPS is urging us to, 'Return to the route'.

One at a time, the wet cop is letting every other stream of cars pass through the intersection. We wait in a silence, which I break. 'Yes, I think I would like a hug. Please.' The cop waves us through the intersection. Theo takes an exit ramp and pulls into a car park under an awning at the back of a twenty-four hour service station. It's almost empty of cars. He turns off the engine and thereby the GPS, which had begun to urge us to make a U-turn. He reaches over, pulls me as close as the gear stick will allow and simply holds me. I feel my breathing slow. I remember that he just helped save my grandmother and I haven't even thanked him yet. I burrow into his salty-smelling neck and say quietly, 'I haven't even thanked you.'

'The hospital's on my way home anyway,' he replies.

'No. Not for the lift. Well, yes, for the lift too. But for what you did back there.'

'Anyone would do it,' he says.

'I couldn't. I froze. I watched. I was on the edge of it all. Pretty bloody useless.'

'I think it's harder if you're closer to the person,' he says.

'You came to a party where you hardly knew anyone and then pretty much got Yiayia going again. I knew what to do in theory but I didn't know what to do when in the moment.'

'I've done it before,' he says, 'but that time, it didn't work. I can't believe it worked this time.' I shut my eyes and burrow some more. Theo continues talking quietly, 'It was not long before I left. On a construction site. He was a friend. A beam fell on him. He died on the site.

Occupational health and safety is pretty crappy in Athens.' The rain continues to belt down on the awning above us. 'And the ambulance took ages. The paramedics told me that I did all I could have done. That the odds were really stacked against me, but it didn't make me feel any better.'

'I'm sorry.' It's all I can think to say. I open my eyes and retreat from my burrow. My eyes are level with his dark eyebrows, which are no longer acting as bullshit meters. He's got tears in his eyes. I rest my forehead against his and we remain still. Then I kiss him. He responds slowly. It's pure pleasure.

The neon petrol sign at the side of the road is illuminated even more by another flash of lightning. It jolts us and we explore each other more quickly. He reclines his seat. I move with him, helping him to remove his shirt. As the thunder rumbles, a hairy but sexy Greek chest greets me. No waxing here.

'Are you sure?' he asks me. 'We'll arrive even later. Your mother?'

'I'm very sure and I'd like to forget my mother for just this moment.'

If Yiayia's chorus could see this Nice Greek Boy and this Not So Nice Greek Girl now. My fingers trace over his chest. I kiss his eyelids. He's smiling, helping me remove my clothes and kissing every bit of me within his reach.

As more lightning flickers, I tug his jeans down as he reaches his hand into his pocket, searching. He pulls out a condom. So, he'd thought he might get lucky at a Community Club on a rainy Saturday night? That's confidence. But he's hard and I'm wet and next we're fucking furiously. As the rain eases outside, we melt silently into each other.

No thunder. No lightning. No rain on the roof.

In the distance, we see a beefy bloke leave the diner and head towards a rig in one of the big bays behind us. We lie low, handing each other bits of clothing. We somehow manage to get the right bits in the right places. I fumble in my handbag for a cigarette and lighter. 'I'd love one,' he says. 'I'm giving them up in Australia but this is a bit different.'

'Sure,' I reply. 'I'm giving them up in Greece.'

'That might be the worst country in the world to try that. All Greeks smoke.'

We're standing by the car. The truck driver blasts his horn, gives us an exaggerated thumbs-up and heads into the night. We enjoy our nicotine together. 'Well, we'd better do that U-turn,' he says. 'Your mother will be wondering where you are.'

'Would you come into the hospital with me?' I ask.

'Your Mum is a bit scary. I don't want to get in her way and I'm not so good at looking a mother in the eye when I've just had sex with her daughter.'

'Avoid all eye contact,' I direct.

Peia

Shapes, beeps, tubes and dreams.

Theío Angel with Mama on our balcony. 'Tell me a story about Salonika,' she says. 'Do you remember the first time you visited us by yourself?' he asks.

Mama replies, 'You and Theía Beth were at the port waiting for me. As we walked, Theía Beth started crying. You told me that Theía Beth is always sad when she walks past her old home, which had been destroyed in a huge city fire but that there was no way to reach your new home without passing her old one.'

'You hugged Theía Beth,' he says, 'and you told her, "While I am here I will find a way for you to reach your new home without having to pass your old one." You never did find a way.'

Has Teo come back because I can't live in my new home without having to go past my old one?

Mama says, 'The next morning, we went walking. In one neighbourhood, I saw huge homes—blue, pink and ochre—they stared at me with enormous empty eyes. In another place, similar homes, bursting with life. A woman greeted Theía Beth who had delivered her babies. The woman said, "These people just moved into our home. They are planning to stay and we must go".'

Then we headed towards the White Tower. The market was full of life. Around the wharves, people were waking up. Theío Angel says, 'You were staring at a family that wanted to get on one of the ships. A woman was trying to sell some pots to a local who was bargaining her down. You wanted us to intervene on the seller's behalf. You were cranky that we wouldn't. If we had bought all the pots from all of the women at the wharf, our home would have been full of pots and we would have had no room for you.'

Jo

But never, never on a Sunday, a Sunday, a Sunday, 'Cause that's my day of rest.

It's one o'clock in the morning on Easter Sunday, at least according to the clock ticking slowly and staring down at me from above the sleek, silver vending machine. I do not know what to ask of it. Next to the vending machine is a huge painted forest wall mural. According to a plaque, it was painted by a teacher and group of students from a local high school. It is rather good. Mostly eucalyptus trees. Mama would approve. She loves forests. Perfect for hiding in, she says. Tall trees with soft leaves dominate. I swear I can smell peppermint and lemon. Blue sky is peeking through the clouds but only a little. There is the trace of a walking track and a shrub understorey. So many shades of green. Fern. Jungle. Mint. Artichoke. Moss. Pine. Teal. Avocado. Olive. And flecks of black-green, silver-green and yellow-green. It is the hard, dry leaves that draw me in. Maybe each class member painted their own shrub? What shrub would my school-self have painted? A dark one, I think.

Da is dozing in a chair nearby. His twinkling eyes are hooded. The fluorescent hospital lights highlight the few grey strands in his red hair. Anna is late, whatever 'late' is at this ungodly hour. Just this once she could have been on time. She has never missed a deadline at work, but there is no time triage in her personal life. What could possibly be more important to her right now?

I keep seeing Mama's face. Well, her two faces. The one that was paralysed and the one that was crying. Peia's girls don't cry. She led the fundraising for the defibrillator. A galaktoboureko drive. Acres of filo pastry lined her kitchen benches. Tonnes of cream and butter. Dozens of eggs. But at this moment, there is not an Easter egg in sight in the accident and emergency ward.

Anna needs to be at the airport by four o'clock if she is to catch her seven o'clock flight. Where is she? She should be with me here on the midnight shift. Every bit of me is scared about my life without her. About the next bit of my life, which was meant to be my bit to spend as I wished.

Losing weight. Exercising. Yoga. Painting. Proper painting. Visiting Anna in Greece. When will I get my bit?

They have taken Mama for some scans. To assess the extent of 'the damage'. She can recover. Knowing Mama, she will recover. That is what I should tell Anna. But Mama's face. Her paralysis. Her tears.

I have friends who have dealt with their parents' strokes. But the patience. The positive thinking. The three steps forwards and four steps back. Mama will not like this dance. It is not on her time and I will not have Anna to help me.

Anna seems distant already as she walks slowly towards me down the long linoleum hallway. Theo is trailing behind her, reading every hospital sign. Why is he here? And now I am crying. Years of tears gush down my face. They are coming from way, way down in me. My heart is racing and I am shaking. Da stirs and turns towards me. He stretches out his arms and I fall into them. A heaving mess: great big me and little old him. I do not need Theo to witness this moment.

Anna sees us and stops, some distance away. She talks to Theo and pulls her phone out of her handbag. Should she be using it in here? I slump down in the seat next to Da's and wipe my eyes. Anna and Theo are now moving together along the blue-and-white tiled floor. They pass several banks of utilitarian white chairs, seating other grief-stricken families, some of whom are receiving explanations from blue-and-white clad staff. Anna and Theo stop next to an abandoned laundry trolley nearby. Theo heads straight towards the mural and touches it. He then checks out the vending machine. Perhaps he knows what to ask of it? Anna sits down opposite us.

'You are late,' I say. Anna raises her eyebrows and appears to be about to say something. I add, 'But she is okay.'

'Then why were you crying?' she asks.

'Must be the relief,' I hear myself lie. 'Can I see her?' she asks.

'They are doing some follow-up tests,' I reply. 'Just to be sure to be sure,' says Da, smiling.

She is flicking through her phone. 'I'll cancel my ticket.' 'Why?' I ask.

'Because Yiayia's had a stroke and you two don't look so great,' she answers.

'Nobody looks great in Accident and Emergency after midnight,' says Da, 'and she wouldn't want you to stay because of her. Yiayia will be fine and so will me and your mum. Won't we, Jo Jo?'

She stares at us both and asks, 'How can I possibly go?'

'Anna, you told me they want you now,' I say. 'Heaps of other people applied for the job, presumably one of them will be offered it if you do not turn up.'

A slow Da edges towards Anna and speaks to her in his softest lilt. 'Yiayia wants you to go to Greece and she wants to hear all about your adventures.' For the second time tonight, he is begging a woman he loves to do something. One to stay. One to go.

'I can take Anna home to get her bag and then to the airport,' offers Theo, staring at the mural. 'I haven't got any plans for the next few hours.'

'Mum, I really need to see her, can you ask?'

Peia

Voices and machines hum. Like summer bees in a forest. There's no pain now but there's been miles of movement. I haven't moved but others have moved me. Some sore movement like when Teo moved faster than me. New rooms. New faces. The warmth is manufactured here. I blink and see some coloured blankets spread across my legs.

I'm here but I'm not here. I'm also not sure where 'here' is.

Someone is moaning. Soft voices are speaking to me. I'm sure that the voices are asking me questions but as I think about maybe finding some words to answer a question, the letters for that answer get stuck and then my mind tells me it is easier to go back. Way, way back to the forest on that day. It's easier to be there than to be here. Wherever 'here' is. It's easier to sleep than stay awake.

There we were. Here I am.

A noise startles me. I see a child. I should smile but my face cannot fully commit to doing so.

A little girl. Sitting on my knee. Summer again. She was a fussy eater. I tried every trick in the world to get her to eat green things. We had a book. We made a game. She says, 'I am Anna, Anna I am.'

I say, 'Does Anna like green veg and lamb?'

She says, 'I do not like green veg but lamb. I'd rather like some ram and lamb.'

I say, 'Would you like it here or there?'

Here or there? That's the thing. I'm not here or there. Is the little girl here or there? There's something about her being here or there. I think she wants to go there. I'm from there. I can't go there now. Something is weighing me down. Have I helped her get to there? She should go there. Should she go there?

'Peia, your daughter is here. Can you tell me your daughter's name?' Another question. Some letters come out. I hope I've answered correctly. 'Peia, is this your daughter?' I nod. I hope it is my daughter.

We are on a holiday and sitting under some cypress trees. We are with other families but this little round girl is just plain cranky today and won't talk or play with anyone. Not with the children or the adults. Not even with Mórai Josephine.

The person, who I think is my daughter, says some words. 'Greece. Today. Anna.'

Grown-up Teo is here. He's not that little boy running away this time. I stretch out my hand and the person I think is my daughter takes it. Teo's letters come out of my mouth. The one I think is my daughter removes her hand from mine. She is white. She turns to a man with red-grey hair seated in a chair. He takes her hand. The man I think is Teo then takes one of my hands in his two hands. Tears on my face. Tears on his face? The other little girl is next to him. I have something for her. Something for her to take from here to there. Come on letters. 'Agb. Gba. Abg. Bga. Gab. Bag.'

The person I think is my daughter says, 'Bag?'

I nod. Some movement. The large white person I think is my daughter goes to a bedside cupboard. She removes my handbag and places it next to me on the bed. The other girl, the one I think wants to go from here to there, opens it and starts pulling things out. My hanky? No. My purse? No. My notebook? No. My worry beads? Yes. My special worry beads. The ones with two interlocking rings. One ring has the beads and the other ring has a kangaroo with a joey in its pouch. She places them in my left palm. I hold them tight and then I place them in her right palm. Letters and words rise up and come out. 'Here to there. With them.'

Anna

It's nearly three o'clock in the morning. Theo surveys my small unit. 'Do you want me to clean up a bit for your friend while you get ready?'

'It's not dirty.'

'I could just clear the sofa and dining table. Give her room to put some stuff?'

'She's messy too. She won't mind. She's happy to have the place.'

'Maybe I could just wash those dishes in the sink?'

'Fine. I'll have a quick shower and change.'

'Would you like a coffee?' he asks.

'Yes. There's a machine. There should be some pods somewhere.'

The hot water gushes down on me. I try to savour it, ahead of the long haul flight. But Yiayia looked so sick and sad. Mum was white and weeping and Daddo was trying to please everyone.

I grab my towel from the floor and wrap it around me. It's wet and doesn't provide me with what I need. I'm equivocating in a cold wet towel. I've said goodbye to Mum, Yiayia and Daddo. I have their words in my head. They did what they thought was the right thing. They let me go.

I hear Theo's voice. 'I can't find any pods. Got any instant?' '

I'm sure there are pods somewhere.'

Clothes for the plane? Clothes that I can sleep in that won't look slept in. I head to my room through the living area. Theo stands next to a pile of shining crockery that's been stacked on the sink. It could be a dishwashing detergent advertisement, except for the Greek boy.

'I had to give up on coffee,' he announces, looking straight at me in my wet towel. No time for diversions.

'The pods might be at the back of the fridge.' A clear, practical response. I keep moving. I'd forgotten I had put the comfy clothes on my bed, ready to go. I throw on a clean everything and head back out.

The coffee machine is groaning. 'There's no milk,' he says.

'I have it black. Strong.'

'There's no sugar.'

'I don't take sugar.'

He hands me a coffee and asks, 'Do you need a hug?'

'I don't have time for another hug.'

'A hug-hug?'

'Coffee's good. I need to get going.'

He's now clearing my dining table. 'Still want to go?' he asks.

'Yes.' I riffle through my plane backpack to check that I've got everything. 'You seem more undecided about going since the hospital visit.'

Right now, I don't want to hear his thoughts or answer his questions. 'Yiayia gave me her kangaroo and joey. If that isn't a green light, I don't know what is.' *Here to there. With them.* Her words echo in my head as I stare at my passport photograph. I look so young.

'I think you're worried about your mum.'

'Mum always copes. She's like Yiayia in that way.'

'So, it's a good deal for your mum?'

'Why are you suddenly worried about my mum?'

'Well, I just left mine behind, which I don't feel so great about. And I think I might have said my final goodbye to my yiayia.

'So, I should stay to help you get over your guilt about your mother and grandmother?'

'I could help you look after all of them.'

'So, I stay so we can start an aged-care outreach organisation?'

He moves to the sink. 'Got a clean tea towel?'

'There's a mostly clean one on the hook over there.'

He holds it up to the light and then starts drying the dishes. A book for the flight. I bought a new one. Where is it? He turns around, tea towel in hand. 'Late last night, your grandmother received lifesaving emergency medical care. She wouldn't have got that in Athens. Why do you want to go to some idealised version of Greece that she brought you up on?'

'Because I speak some Greek and I live in a small bubble in Australia.' I find my book.

'Well, you'll get a very different bubble in Greece. Austerity for five years in a row now. The idyllic Greece the old people talk about doesn't exist anymore, if it ever existed. Greece is dire. If you want to do the international journalist thing, why not go somewhere worth saving to strut your stuff?'

Worth saving? To strut my stuff? I ignore him. Sleeping mask. Sleeping mask. I find it in a bathroom drawer. I head to my backpack. 'It's not about "*saving places*" or "*strutting my stuff*", I need to get out of here.'

'Fine, but why go there? Now?'

'Because this is my big chance.' Where is my neck pillow? I usually file it under my bed, so I head there on my quest. I lie on the floor, headfirst, under my bed and there is Theo, lying on his stomach on the opposite side.

'Greece is hopeless. The government is useless. Unemployment is over twenty per cent. I'm never going back.'

I see my neck pillow. It's seen better days but it will do. I reverse out. Now, Theo and I are both standing on opposite sides of the bed. 'Theo, okay, we fucked, but you knew I was going.' He grabs my now empty coffee cup from the floor and heads to the living room. I follow him. 'Theo, we've known each other for five minutes as adults. It's one minute to midnight and I need to get to the airport.' I tie my neck pillow to my backpack. I think I have everything. Theo is taking ages to wash one coffee mug. 'Theo, if all this is a bit too hard, I can get an Uber to the airport.'

'Don't be stupid. You'll be late.'

'That wouldn't be a first.'

'I should drop you off. I told your mother I would.'

I grab my stuff. Pause. Think. On my final check of my backpack, I sense and see a joey, staring straight through me.

Peia

My sleep was dark dreams. Words won't come to my lips but they are jumping around in my head. Where is Harry?

Lypiménos. Sad.

Melancholikós. Depressed.

Sad puddle. *Melancholikós* mire. 'Patient is over there,' a voice says.

A White Coat pointing at me. I can see and hear. 'Where's the nurse?' the White Coat asks.

'Here I am and here are the notes.' The nurse (?) takes my hand.

White Coat: 'Stroke … support team … up and running as soon as possible … ischemic … reduced blood flow.'

Iskhein. Keeping back. *Haima*. Blood.

I couldn't keep back Teo's blood. Did anyone keep back his blood? A buzzer. White Coat goes. Nurse goes too.

Alone. No team. I shut my eyes. The girl who went from here to there said *Do not hurry the journey at all.*

Sigà, sigà: Slowly, slowly is for the good times. I hate slow now.

White Coat's voice again.

'Brain injured … few more tests … weakness right side.'

Both my sides used to be so strong.

My hand receives another squeeze. The nurse? My tears are being wiped.

'Start rehabilitation in the next day or so.'

Why would I start? I don't have the energy.
Apaisiodoxía. Pessimism.

Jo

A long day has followed a long night. Da and I are with Maysa, the rehabilitation coordinator, having visited Mama who recognised Da but not me. 'It's normal,' she explains. 'Patients can also have problems with object recognition.' At the moment I would be quite happy to be recognised as an object by Mama.

Móraí Josephine always recognised me and was at my birth. She helped Theía Beth. 'Beth was like flowing water by name and by nature,' Móraí Josephine always said. 'For forty-five years, she delivered babies and her mother did the same, forty-five years before her in Saloniki.'

'What's next?' Da asks. He's much more in the moment than I am.

'The tests this morning explored the weakness on her right side. She has hemiplegia, which is some, but not full, incapacitation there.' I must be part of the 'some incapacitation'.

Móraí Josephine said that a funny part of my birth was that the top of my head popped out and in, out and in, like a mouse in a hole. Beth said, 'This one is really not so sure about coming out to meet the world.' My head-popping indecision apparently went on for several minutes. Until Theía Beth murmured, 'I'm not playing cat and mouse with you.' The next time, she was ready. She cupped my head with one hand until my neck emerged and then she scooped me up with her other hand as more of me emerged. She handed me to my crying mother, who kissed me and said, 'Welcome to the world Josephine Anna the second.'

Maysa again. 'It's a pity you missed the doctor on his rounds this morning.' We missed the doctor this morning because Da wanted to go to church again today and he needed me to take him. His Mass consisted of him kneeling, holding his head in his hands, while mine consisted of an excess of lighting of candles. Maysa continues speaking, 'We take a team approach to rehabilitation and work closely with the patient and the family.'

There was a team at my birth.

Maysa stays on point. 'I should be clear, the rehabilitation won't cure her, but it will provide her with the chance to achieve the best possible quality of life.' She is in fact very clear. Mama will not dance back to what she was once before.

'What will actually happen with her?' enquires Da.

'She should be able to relearn a lot of skills. Some might not come back, but with persistence she should be able to learn other ways of doing things.' Persistent she is, but she is very set in her way of doing things, which will mean more battles for me.

'How soon will it all start?' asks Da.

'We'll start with helping her move her limbs while she's in bed. Maybe sitting up in bed, then moving herself from the bed to a chair, then maybe from a chair to standing up. Eventually, hopefully, she'll get enough confidence to do things like feed herself, shower herself and go to the toilet.'

'Mama's confidence comes from climbing mountains, not going to the toilet,' I burst out.

Maysa pauses before continuing. 'It's really important that we get her feeling good about doing some basic things first.' Mama's basic needs will be so different to my basic needs.

Da asks, 'How long will she be in hospital?'

'We'll move her as soon as possible to our inpatient rehabilitation unit, where she will probably stay for several weeks. It's an intensive program.'

Maysa seems to be implying that things will be more intensive than now. Things are already intensive enough for me. 'And after that?' I ask.

'Depending on her progress and a home assessment, she may become an outpatient.' Mama as an outpatient. I am not coping with her as an inpatient. Maysa continues, 'Stroke recovery can be a long journey, depending on the extent of the brain damage.' Da takes in this information.

Mórai Josephine said that, after my birth, she just sat on the side of the bed falling in love with me and then Theía Beth spat on me lightly three times. 'Just casting out the evil eye,' Theía Beth announced. 'If we all do it three times each, it will be even more powerful,' she added.

Maysa, Da and I need to spit on Mama now. Maysa's voice interrupts my reverie. 'Some, not many, words are coming out but generally they are in the wrong order. Who is Teo? It's a name that comes out clearly and quite regularly.'

Da looks at me before answering. 'Teo was her younger brother. He's presumed dead. Something happened when she was about fifteen, before she came to Australia.'

I am fifty-five years old and I have just learned something very new. Teo is not Theo. Mama is not just confused. The three sentences Da delivered to Maysa contained three bits of the Mama puzzle that I should have known long before today. She should have told me. He should have told me. I hold my head in my hands and try to steady my thoughts.

The room is quiet but for the background of hospital din. As I raise my head, Maysa speaks softly while looking at me. 'With strokes it's not unusual for all sorts of memories to bubble up.'

Bubble. Such a soft image. Mama's bubbles are anything but soft. 'Is she in any physical pain?' I ask.

'No, not at the moment but in all likelihood she will experience some pain during rehabilitation. It's hard work.'

I hope the pain she feels is at least equivalent to mine at this moment.

Da speaks again to both of us. 'She is sad. Very sad.'

Maysa responds. 'Yes, she is and that too is not unusual. A stroke is a huge shock to the system. Has she had any depression before?'

Da looks directly at me before he turns to Maysa. 'Not that Jo would remember, but yes, she did have a major episode when she first arrived in Australia.'

To me Mama has always been tinged with depression, Da but, as you rightly say, I did not see the first episode in Australia.

Peia

The two little boys playing upstairs have cabin fever. Their mothers are out working in the muddy fields away from our home. I am acting as an alchemist in our kitchen, expanding scant winter food into miraculous meals; we are sending most of what we produce on the farm to our army. The two little boys sound as though they are climbing the walls. I stand captivated by the smells and sight of my fasolada. I am relishing my loaves and fishes moment. No actual loaves or fishes, but white beans, carrots, onions and celery. The soup will feed us all for several days.

Now, I am moving to check on the boys. They are not climbing the walls but the steep banisters. They are at the top of the very top balustrade. Adelphos is helping Teo to lie face downwards on the balustrade, arms first, head first, stomach to stair rail. Adelphos is calling out, 'One. Two. Three. Go!' Teo is flying towards me. Still attached to the wood but winged. Somehow, I am suddenly where I need to be. Teo is still flying towards me.

Body join up. Unlock. Arms do your thing. Release. Catch. I hook him. We are falling. We are laughing, the sound is a declaration of Teo's safe delivery. We are hugging. Adelphos is yoking himself to us. Now, it is just three relieved bodies breathing as one ball. Calmed cabin fever this time but I'll have to get them out of here or it will be a very long day with tears before bedtime.

From beyond our cypress tree the forest sirens call to us.

Anna

On the train, on the way from the airport last night, a well-groomed and smartly dressed older American man standing next to me was silently robbed. He'd given his seat to a young woman and child as the train got fuller and we were approaching central Athens. They exited one stop later while we were talking. He didn't even feel the money leaving his body. Travelling alone had made me a bit desperate for a chat. Him too apparently.

The night guy on the desk at my hotel took my money but not my bag. I felt every one of its kilograms as I dragged it up six flights of narrow threadbare stairs to greet my small room on the top floor.

Both these events have heightened my sense of being alone. I didn't think I would feel like this in Yiayia's home. I thought I'd feel more connected. Bloody Odysseus. Curled into a small ball and clutching a carved kangaroo and joey, I cried myself into a sleep, which was constantly interrupted by my last images of Mum, Daddo, Yiayia and Theo.

It's been less than twenty-four hours since my departure and I can hear Mum's words, 'Athens wasn't built in a day'. In the brief time that I've spent in my room, I've felt love (as I craned my neck out the small window and glimpsed the night-lit Acropolis), hate (for the night watchman), highs (that Yiayia was still alive for me) and lows (over the extra money I'd paid for a very cold shower, which was very little like a shower and much more like a washing machine hose, and the subsequent spread of water across my floor).

I'm now seated at a port-side café. My train ride to the café contrasted starkly to that of my train ride from the airport last night. The train today was mostly full of locals going about their day. I am soaking up the port's air, blue and space when a barrier of unchained cruisers crosses my bow. Scary in their bright parallel universe but tourism marches on.

Sitting in a corner booth, I feel even smaller when a larger-than-life legendary Greek woman strides towards me. It's Ani, my new boss, who obviously functions on Greek time. She booms, 'Anna. Anna. *Sygnómi, Sygnómi, Kalimera, Kalimera.*'

It's almost Kalispera, but I call back enthusiastically, 'Kalimera.'

No questions asked, she orders Greek coffee for both of us. It arrives almost before she's finished ordering. She squeezes in opposite me and leans forwards, her breasts taking up much of the table. Her huge black oval glasses are held up by her two smiling cheeks. I'm nervous that she might pinch my not-so-smiling ones. 'So,' she says, 'Anna, we should eat too.' She broadcasts another order and suddenly a mound of pastries sits between us, their fresh smell tainted just a little by the waiter's strong cologne. 'We'll eat and talk,' she says enthusiastically, pointing to the pastries. I take one from the top of the mound and she takes the next. 'Ready for it?' she asks.

'Well, I slept through breakfast, so yes.'

'Not the food. The job. The adventure. Life.'

'Absolutely. Can't wait,' I answer through a mouthful of custard. 'I have …'

'I'm so sorry,' she interrupts. 'How is your yiayia?'

'Not great, but not worse.'

She points outside to the sea that today is postcard Greek blue. 'This is my patch. Where was your yiayia born?' she asks.

'In the north. The mountains. Saloniki was her nearest city,' I respond.

'My soul seeks the sea. My *pappoú* ran coasters around the Aegean and Mediterranean. His Papa sailed wooden trading *caïques* through the islands. My papa preferred the whole world for his fleet. My sister runs the business now. Papa's world has shrunk a little. Not the best of shipping times but still afloat. Your yiayia, which village?'

I'm stumped with custard stuck between my teeth. 'I'm not sure. It was small.' 'Well, that would cover most of them.'

I've spent my professional life asking and answering the right questions at the right time. Why am I unable to do so now when I really need to?

She grabs another pastry and makes an expansive arm gesture. 'This is my family's other office. See that door there? We celebrate out there; do business in here.'

Since Yiayia's stroke, I've been at sea in a skiff. My personal life is poking my professional life and I hate it. There's a child crashing around in my head. 'I'm very excited to be working with you,' I throw in, custard-free. 'Chance of a lifetime.' God, where did that come from?

She pauses mid-pastry. 'So, what does a "chance of a lifetime" look like to you?'

Out of nowhere, Theo's bullshit eyebrow barometer rises and falls before me. Get this right. Please get this right. 'I want to learn everything I can from you,' I answer.

She pulls out a packet of cigarettes and offers one to me. I point to the non-smoking sign above her.

'Yes?' she queries. I take one and she lights us up and inhales deeply. The waiter delivers an ashtray. 'So many young Greeks want to go to Australia for their chance of a lifetime and yet you leave their chance of a lifetime to take your chance here. Why so?'

'I want to work on substantial stories. International ones.'

'I can give you *substantial.* Plenty of it. There's no shortage of Ani-projects. You'll start working on some tomorrow when you meet the others.' She smokes with one hand and finishes eating her pastry with the other. 'You'll start with my ideas, but to do substantial work in this business you have to have your own ideas; ideas that excite you, that bring out your passion.

In Greece and in documentary making, you can't be tepid about anything.' She has seen straight through to my tepidity. As I am trying to conjure up a non-tepid something to say, she asks, 'Has anything interesting happened to you since you arrived?'

'Not really,' I answer. 'Well, an old guy I was chatting to on the train got robbed.'

'How did you follow that up?' she asks.

A tepid puddle dribbles out. 'I didn't really. I wished him well.'

Our coffee cups are refilled as she continues. 'Do robberies on trains happen all the time in Australia?'

'Not near me. Not regularly. No.' I don't have time to account for my three tepid responses in a row before she fires her next questions.

'So, what happened on the train was maybe linked to a story? To migration and why so many young Greeks are leaving here for their chance of a lifetime? To economic hard times, poverty and unemployment?' The professional has snookered the amateur. 'Everything you do here and everyone you meet is research. We'll put the missed story of the guy on the train down to tiredness and your yiayia's illness.' Her eyes become magnified as she speaks, 'When people come to Greece they always want to see the ruins. In my company, we dig for stories, way down beyond the top layers of a site. So many layers it's not always obvious, but then the site joins up.' She grabs another pastry with her spare hand, deposits it into my spare hand and takes one for herself. I hold mine like an extra glove. 'So,' she says, inhaling, 'say "yes" to every opportunity while you're here. You'll get tired, you'll get bored, you'll get frustrated and homesick but everything is an opportunity to make great stories.'

We finish our cigarettes and I move my uneaten pastry to my mouth hoping it might stop any more bullshit from coming out. 'But practical things now. Here's Sinead's number. She's in the team and has a spare room in her apartment. Contact her today to see if that could work.' I take the piece of paper and thank her. She stands looking down at me for a moment and then exits as energetically as she entered. Everything goes on a tab and I am a sardine in her wake as I receive a text from Theo. '*Are you there yet*?'

Peia

Last night I had the dream that won't submit. I tell it to go away but it lures me in every time with a feast. I can't resist a feast. The first time, I was drawn in by a duet of saganaki cheese and dolmas. The next time, a trio of greens, zucchini flowers and beans convinced me to sit down with them and Teo and Adelphos. Last night, there was a rabbit surrounded by sausages and a magical setting near a mountain lake. That feast. That last supper where we agreed to the plan that you make in terrible times when there is no other plan to make.

Harry is reading to me. Grace O'Malley, a princess and a pirate. She did what she had to do in terrible times. When there are no good options.

When I first arrived in Australia and was living with Theío Angel, Harry's mother, Josephine (often with Harry and his younger sister Frankie) would sit me down in our combined back garden and read me Irish stories to help me with my English. During that time, I fell in love not only with the epic stories but also with Harry, Josephine's lilt and Frankie's irreverence.

Harry reads, 'Grace's name brings us the sounds of soft music.'

Harry has been the soft music to my demanding dance.

There is no dance in my dream but a children's play. 'Odysseus and the Cyclops'. There's me whimpering in the dark, near the forest. *Haima.* Blood. No *iskhein.* No blood stopping. Blood flowing. In me and out of me. My nose is red; my feet are all webby; my eyes are bruised. My neck is scrawny. My feathers are dank and clumpy. My noises get louder and louder and redder and redder. I pray that for every strike I endure the boys will run further and further away.

Is it another Sunday?

On Sunday mornings, after Mass, it was open house at our place. Frankie playing the piano. Harry playing his fiddle, with no coaxing necessary. Padraig and other parishioners dropping by, eating and declaring Josephine's scones the best in Christendom.

In good weather, we all spilled into the back garden. Theía Beth and Theío Angel hosted a similar open house next door. The Roman Catholic and Greek Orthodox congregations mixed happily enough together under a unifying grape vine, with tea and scones and coffee and baklava. A Greek-style Sunday roast, with lashings of lemon, followed for family and any hangers-on who wished to stay.

Sometimes, there would be a loud knock from the laneway on Theío Angel's shed door and, under the garlic, he'd welcome someone. When I arrived here, he and Theía Beth brought me to their home through the shed. They wanted me to feel some of Greece in their back garden. He would always let me join him with others who were trying to find loved ones.

'Good morning.'

'Good morning.'

'How are you?'

'Very well. Thank you. You?'

'Well. Thank you.'

After the international Greek greetings had been completed over coffee, the guests would beg Theío Angel with great passion to help them find someone they'd lost. The boys I lost are visiting me every night. 'I will try, I will try!' Theío Angel always declared.

I should declare that I'll try. Grace O'Malley convinced the Queen of England to give her back her life but I have aphasia and am not sure I want my life. Another Greek word. *A*-not. *Phanai*-speak. I can't design what sounds come out, so I'm not putting in much effort.

When I learned most of my English in Australia, I put in so much effort. But my forgotten past has decided to come back now and is jumping out when I don't want it to jump out. I just want some normal to come out

Harry reads, 'A great wave carried Grace's vessel up on its crest.'

A crest will rise if I say more than four words like they say I did the night Anna left. They like hope. I like silence.

Harry again, 'I would have rolled off the vessel like a helpless log had she not put forth her hand and caught mine.'

Teo was a helpless log in a cavernous forest. Did someone put forth their hand?

But I would like to say 'Harry' and deep down I see his letters. His name should come up and out as long as I start with the soft sounds and work up to the two '*r*' letters. Come up, 'Harry'. The letters are deep down. Come up to my mouth, letters. 'Hhhrrrppp' comes out. I sound like a pig but Harry stops, smiles and strokes my throat.

My father and mother gave me Teo and I lost him, but I found Harry. Breathe more slowly. Like in the dance. But dancing isn't as exhausting as this is.

In the dark, it's worse. Just me and my call button. Burp words become whimpers. It returns me to the whimpering dark near the forest where the noises got louder and louder and I got redder and redder and the little boys ran further and further away.

I have heard story after story of inspiring modern stroke heroes. They have not moved me. Why do these ancients move me so?

I just need to say 'Harry'. I want to non-burp 'Harry'. Something is rising in my throat. Could be Harry's letters. But whatever is there is stuck. Jumbled. 'Hare'. 'Harry'. '*Leípei*'.

'Missing'. 'Me'. '*Mou*'. Harry is missing from me. But there he is by my side. Reading to me. The music to my dance.

Anna

We pass thousands of people carrying placards as we try to get close to the Finance Minister at the May Day march in central Athens. If he can pull Greece out of this one, Australia no doubt will claim that his time spent down-under was key.

I haven't escaped the Irish. With me, behind the camera, is our Lisbeth Salander look-alike, Sinead from Shannon. Her tattoo is a red carnation. She's twenty-five years old and in her move to Greece she is seeking to replace tourism marketing in the west coast of Ireland with some gutsy story making. She is sharing her apartment with me. Daddo was delighted to hear the news; he reasons that I'm safe if I'm with the Irish.

Another placard, or rather a very large protestor holding a placard, blocks our path. As we jostle our way towards the front, Sinead yells at me, 'We should be more careful what we wish for.' It's a sea of megaphones and anti-austerity banners. Ferries to the Aegean islands have been cancelled today. The seamen are holding a twenty-four hour strike to resist the threat of more pension cuts and labour market reforms. On the sidelines, I see some tourists (either brave or naïve) wheeling their suitcases in and out of hotels. As I watch them, I wonder which Syntagma Square hole-in-the-wall was Theo's favourite. I must ask him. Sinead and I have checked out a few.

Greek flags, red flags and yellow visibility vests dominate among men and women, young and old, many of whom look war weary. Little children sit on their fathers' shoulders just as they do at our footy matches back home. This is my first big chance to show Ani that I can capture a key moment in a substantial international story. I ask one of these dads if he'll talk to us. He agrees as his toddler picks at his beard. 'Why are you here today?' I ask.

He thinks a little and then answers, 'For this little boy on my shoulders.'

It's a great reply; he's a bit of a natural. I keep going, as his toddler starts picking at his ear hairs. 'What does the government need to do?' I ask.

'The government needs to argue for more money from the bailout funds or things will get even worse. I fear for the worst.'

'What would the worst be?' I ask.

'Greece is David and the European Union is Goliath. The worst will occur when the government fails to meet its promises to both and Goliath wins instead of David.'

I'm not sure what would be the worst for me but landing back in Australia with my tail between my legs would be close. Can the Greeks beat Goliath? Their consistent response is: 'We're small, we've had it tough for years and we need more time and money'. David never whined about his size or situation. Sinead zooms in on the now smiling toddler. We thank our interviewee and move forwards. We get near enough to the front to see and hear the Finance Minister who, clothed in a black leather jacket, is telling the demonstrators that the working class is alive and well and rediscovering its voice. He's a clever, charismatic guy but he'll need to do more than just speak.

We decide we have enough to go with and begin to walk with others along the crowded streets. Finally, we stop at our vine-covered little bit of Ireland in Athens. I grab a table on the cobblestones outside the pub as Sinead goes inside to get some drinks. The plan is to meet Jimmi and Ani who have been over in

Exarcheia where the nationwide 2008 riots started. It's the graffiti and 'Fuck the World' epicentre of Athens, where the left of the left hangs out. When there aren't riots, it has a great, grungy vibe. Ani wanted to go there today. She doesn't do much frontline work these days. She must have decided to take Jimmi under her wing.

Jimmi arrives, panting, as Sinead plonks down four beers. 'Brilliant timing,' he declares, knocking back half a glass before he even sits down.

'Where's Ani?' I ask him.

'Gone back to the office but not before reminding me why we are all here and working for her.'

'Let me have a go,' I say. I stretch my arms across the table and grab Sinead's black glasses, fiddling them into place on my now smiling cheeks. 'Jimmi, why are we here?' I ask as Ani.

'To make great stories about Greek people.' 'Which Greek people, Jimmi?

'All Greek people, Ani. Greek people here and the Greek diaspora.' He adds a critique, 'You need bigger boobs.'

'We'll have to go with what I've got,' I say, leaning forwards. I turn to Sinead, adjusting her glasses on my cheeks. 'Sinead, why do we care about the diaspora?'

Sinead replies in her fullest west coast Irish accent, 'Like all the great words of the world, it's a Greek word. It means '*to scatter about*'. Greeks are scattered all over the world with their culture and their stories.'

I pause. I look at Jimmi (now downing Ani's beer) and then Sinead before adding, 'And because Greeks are the world's greatest professional migrants.'

They both laugh and then Sinead says, 'Ani, I'm not so sure I agree with you on that. We Irish have got the numbers to be included in the world's honour roll of professional migrants.'

A group walks by with, what looks like, a grandmother in a wheelchair. A woman, perhaps her daughter, pushes the wheelchair intently and seriously, while a younger woman talks on her phone. And here I am, sitting and having a beer and making fun of my boss.

Jimmi orders more beers and pulls out his phone. 'Mind you, Ani and I got up close and personal with Greeks and Molotov cocktails this morning and she did it all like another day at the office.'

He shows us footage of an Athens suburban spring street with burning blue wheelie bins in the middle. Cars are parked at the curbs and tables covered with big umbrellas can be seen on one side of the plaza. The locals continue to go about their business: shopping, having coffee and chatting on their phones. Jimmi's footage also shows masked and hooded cocktail throwers, dressed in summer shorts and joggers, aiming their petrol bombs like targeting baseball pitchers; curving the bombs around people, cars, bicycles, motor bikes and taxis. The traffic lights just keep doing their thing, changing from green to red. Sirens can be heard as riot police with shields enter and scatter the people. The bins keep burning.

Before I left Australia I covered a school fete. It was a favour for a colleague who had nephews at the school. He'd promised he'd try to get something published but got called away to cover a more important story. I went along on a beautiful summer Saturday evening to a leafy street, not dissimilar to the one in front of me in Jimmi's footage. People were sitting around enjoying food and drinks. There was a talent quest and the act that brought the house down involved two boys, aged about ten. These amateur stand-up comedians pitched balls from two blue wheelie bins over which they could barely see. Proud parents snapped pictures of them. That was the last time I saw wheelie bins used to such an effect. Somewhere else in the world people were probably queuing to play all sorts of throwing games. The guys in Jimmi's footage would have beaten all of them. The fete finished with a firework display very different to the one now playing in front of me. I couldn't have covered Exarcheia today.

The family group walks back past us. The younger woman texts as she walks, the woman pushing the wheelchair deftly navigates the cobblestones and the grandmother looks straight through me.

Peia

Theo, who appeared the same night that Teo came back, has wheeled me to the community room and is reading to me. My eyes are shut. I can hear the hum of others but I refuse to join the community of stroke 'survivors'.

Aeolus gave me a wallet and therein bound the paths of the blustering winds.

The winds move me in different ways on different days. Sometimes towards life, sometimes away.

Theo's voice interrupts my thoughts. 'Are you awake?' I nod. That's a point against me because if I can answer, I should answer. Apparently, if I keep relying on gestures my words will stay well away. But the winds have not guided me towards life today, so I nod.

'Theía, when you gave Anna the kangaroo, was it a gift of good winds?' he asks. I nod. After my mama and then me, Teo had the kangaroo. He came back to me the night Anna left, so I gave it to her, so the winds would blow her home safely. Theo says. 'I think you can do better than that. I think you can answer that question.' I open my eyes. He is looking into them. I shut them again. He starts reading again.

Odysseus is close enough to home to see it.

I had yielded the ship to my comrades, that we might the sooner reach home.

Comrades can help you. Comrades can betray you.

They loosed the wallet, and all the winds leapt forth, and swiftly bore us away from our home.

I hear Maysa's voice. 'Hello, Peia. Hello, Theo. Sorry to interrupt the story.' I open my eyes. 'I think you might be more comfortable in an armchair. Is it okay to move you?' I nod.

'Theía, is that a "*Yes*"?' It's Theo again. I nod. He sighs and shakes his head. 'Theo, this is a two-person job. I might get you to help me, okay?' asks Maysa. 'Of course,' Theo replies.

Maysa is to my left. Theo to my right. Me in the middle. All facing out. Like a dance. Except that they are standing and I am sitting. On Maysa's 'One, Two, Three', I am moved sideways to my new chair. It's today's achievement without me doing anything. The winds have moved me. 'Theía, is that more comfortable?' asks Theo.

I nod. Then pause. It is so much easier not to try to speak but then some letters rise and I let them out. 'Yes,' I reply. 'Yes.'

He nods slowly, smiles and then wraps his arms around my shoulders. Out of the corner of my eye I see Maysa ticking a box on her clipboard. That's the first tick I have received here. An achievement, awarded for my doing something. Theo opens our book as though nothing has happened. 'Theía, are you ready for the really good bit where Odysseus's wind-leashing mates are turned into pigs?'

'Yes,' I reply and I ponder whether I should fling myself from the ship and perish in the sea or endure in silence and still remain among the living.

Jo

My Sunday evening Skype call with Anna. Her Sunday morning. I have tried a couple of times already. There's her tanned face now. 'Sorry, Mum. Big late night. How are you?'

Maybe one day we'll start a conversation without an apology. 'I'm okay but the only time I've laughed recently is when our Deputy Prime Minister told Johnny Depp and his girlfriend to bugger off back to America with their dogs.'

Her brown shoulders heave as she settles into a deep laugh. 'Aw, Mum you need a cigarette. I've got an ashtray for us.' She holds up her trusty mint tin and I hold up my packet of cigarettes. We click our lighters in perfect synchronisation from our respective balconies.

I inhale deeply. 'Thank you. I've been looking forward to this. What did you get up to last night?'

'Great time at a journalists' bar. So many of them have been reporting on Greece forever, it made me feel very new, but it was an exciting week covering May Day. Ani really liked my report.'

'Well, your grandmother would be proud of your May Day involvement. She is continuing her program of resistance.'

'Mum, she always takes time to come around.'

'Time? How have you suddenly become so wise?' That came out the wrong way.

'I haven't, but I've observed Yiayia for three decades and I think I know her pretty well.' 'So you would know that she had a younger brother.'

She stops mid-inhale. 'What?'

'The Teo-Theo thing. She had a younger brother, Teo. In Greece. Something happened when she was about fifteen, before she came to Australia.'

'All that Teo talk the night I left. So he was, or is, here?' 'He's presumed dead.'

'How old was he?' Anna asks.

'I have not asked, nor was I told.'

'So, something big happened to her before she went to Australia? And you've only just found out?'

'Yes and yes.'

'Shit. That's late-breaking news. How do you feel?'

It is nice that she has asked. 'Pretty crappy. Shocked. And Da knew. So, as well as being angry with her, I am livid with him or would be if I had either the time or the energy. Every day is the same; we go to the hospital after church. I am aiming to pass the church part on to Padraig, as the church will soon be out of candles and I have to go back to work.'

'Mum, you need to look after yourself or you'll be no good for either of them.'

Out of the mouths of babes. 'I have not got time to look after myself and at least the busyness keeps my mind occupied. Everyone who can help is helping. Calandra sings to her. Her other friends try to feed her pureed-Greek everything but I think even they are all feeling like losers in the Battle of Peia.'

'Is Yiayia talking?'

'Mainly in nouns. Her best effort was the night you left. "Here to there. With them." Everyone still tells her everything about their own dramas but there's nothing coming back the other way. We are on Mama's time.'

Anna holds up the kangaroo and joey. 'I take them everywhere with me. They went to Syntagma Square on May Day. Tell her that.'

'Maybe you could tell her that? I was wondering about you and Yiayia having a Skype? It couldn't hurt.'

'Yeah, sure, but I'm not going to lecture my grandmother on how she should be cooperating more in her recovery.'

'I get that, but you might just give her a spark. She certainly needs something. Most days it is like she has just given up.'

'How does she spend her time?'

'When she's not doing rehab exercises with various health professionals, she lies, sleeps and listens to music. She lets Da, Padraig and Theo read to her, but usually only ancient stories involving heroic deaths.'

'Theo's reading to her?'

'Yes, he visits when he can fit it in around his work.'

'Great,' she replies.

'Mama likes him. She sometimes still calls him Teo. He goes along with it.' 'Go, Theo,' Anna responds through a cloud of tobacco. 'How's Daddo?'

'Trying to be positive and encouraging but not getting far either. In their democracy, her vote counts the most.'

'Always has.'

'He thought she would like some music so he brought in some Greek happy tracks at which she screwed up her nose. The only thing she settles with is rembetika. She now listens to the most god-awful mournful Greek resistance dirges ever written.'

'She tried one of them on me when I was little, but I ended up crying so she started happy dancing instead,' Anna says.

'Now, it makes her cry, upsets Da and confuses me. Her psychologist says it's healthy. Enough of here. How's life with Sinead?'

'It's great. She's great. We have a lot of fun together at play and at work; speaking of which, I wish I knew a bit more about Daddo's history. Ironic that the thought occurred to me now I'm in Greece.'

'The night you left you could have found out all about it from Padraig,' I say. 'Mum, life got a bit distracting that night.'

I continue, 'So, for the record, while you are in Greece and interested in your Irishness, Móraí Josephine talked very little about the family history. She said that Australia was no place to dwell on the past.'

Anna responds, 'Ani asks her international recruits to work on a personal story while they are here-a connection with Greece. The story that Sinead is thinking is her family Irish story; however, I think it's probably a pretty tenuous link to Greece.'

'What story are you thinking of telling?' I ask.

'I hadn't thought of much until today but if Yiayia had a brother called Teo who disappeared and/or died here, it could have been towards the end of the Greek Civil War. *The war that never ended*, according to the journos I partied with last night. It's stirred something in me.'

And now in me too, but not in the same way as in Anna, I suspect. Mama's grip on Anna and me is so potent and we're not even proper Greeks. 'I have to go, Mum. We've got some editing to do today. Let me know when you'd like me to Skype Yiayia. Would you like a mint before I go?'

Peia

Teo, Adelphos and I are standing on our top floor balcony. I am pointing out to them where we will head; where Mama and Theía Trenna won't be able to see us as we carry out our covert icy operation. They are dressed in slightly oversized furry coats with caps and scarves. I'm hoping the extra weight will slow them down a little. They look like two bear cubs who haven't grown into their skins. All fur and alert eyes.

The morning frost is still melting off our orange trees. Other trees have a golden autumn colour and will soon shed some weight to toughen up for winter. We pad through our small hallway, all joined together. The boys have sworn to remain silent until we move beyond our natural amphitheatre.

We are in a line now. Teo giggles at his foggy breath, which sets Adelphos off. I glare at them until their laughter subsides. No flowers edge the muddy upwards path, but breaks in the fog reveal bits of the path network weaving through our steep valley. Lunches are cooking. Smells of soups like mine reach us. Combined vegetable scents for which, like a bear pack, we all stop, raise our noses up and sniff. It's a bonus meal and we are all smiling.

The path forks and we follow hoof marks towards the church where the whitewash has a seasonal mouldy and rusty tinge. The church has temporarily lost its beacon status. When the bear cubs see the church fence they become as one and fly over its boundary. A few sheep scatter and I chase the boys round and round the enclosure until the lure of the towering oaks links them to their next playground. Adelphos, slightly taller although slightly younger, leaps the fence and becomes one with the world beyond. I am not worried because I know that he won't want to get too far ahead of Teo whose left shoe I am currently unbuckling from the fence.

I kiss Teo's now unstuck ankle and look up to see a small smiling bear sitting in a borderless container of acorns. Teo jumps on the little bear and purloins its peaked cap for our acorn collection. This game could go on forever. I join them, offering my cap as another container and off they run.

I lie on my back, looking up twenty metres or so. The ground is slippery and cold, but above me is gold. I sink into my body-shaped acorn pit and form a pillow for my head. There is no sun to see but every colour of gold is above me. I'm warming up. Bright yellow leaves dominate, almost blocking the grey sky from poking through. So many shades of yellow. And red. And green. I close my eyes.

'Peia, look at me!' 'Peia, look at me too!'

My eyes open. There is a small Adelphos bear about ten metres above me. Below him at about six metres a Teo bear. Each is precariously balanced on a branch fork. 'I can see the edge of the world,' yells Teo.

'I can see beyond the edge of the world,' counters Adelphos.

'I can see beyond the edge of the world to the edge of the next world,' responds Teo.

'I can see beyond the edge of the world to beyond the edge of the world after the next world,' returns Adelphos.

This game could also go on forever. Adelphos is distracted by a maple seed helicopter floating down towards him. He moves a little to the right, seems to double his furry arm length and captures it in his glove. He is momentarily at one with it. And then he looks down. 'Teo catch this!' he calls. The bright flare is released. Six alert eyes watch its descending progress as Teo's hand moves slightly to cup it.

'It's mine now!' he yells.

The vow of silence has been well and truly broken. And then I hear a donkey on a path nearby. And a woman talking to a donkey. Six eyes connect again. I put one gloved finger to my lips while the finger on my other hand points at that finger. Four cub eyes have seen it. I bury down into my acorn tomb. I have an eye hole.

The woman is talking to the donkey about the day's success in gathering chestnuts. She is telling the donkey that there will be chestnuts cooked on an open fire for supper. I am already salivating, but I salivate even more as she describes the shells splitting open, the soft insides and the anticipated pleasure. Her voice and the donkey's hooves descend into the valley.

I pop my head up and see the very still cubs. I put my finger to my lips again and motion for the boys to climb down. They do so somewhat awkwardly but exceptionally quietly. We regroup and, without talking, head back down. Teo is holding the red helicopter flare as though his life depends on it. At a fork in the path, on one side we see the women still in the field and, on the other side, our cypress tree. Sweet scents are wafting up. A silent and smiling bear pack stops, raises its nose and sniffs it all in. Oranges, almonds and honey. Mission almost accomplished.

Anna

It's Saturday or International Skype Day as it's now also known. At about three o'clock in the morning, I invited Jimmi and Sinead to join me. They are finishing their coffees downstairs. From a purely selfish viewpoint, it means that I won't have to do all the talking, which is particularly important today. Punctual I may be, but I have been up all night.

Mum's arranged a big screen at the other end in the community room and I'm at our office on another big screen. Ani told me it was fine to use the equipment for a diasporic conversation. I wave as I see Mum in a room full of murals. I'll bet she's critiqued every one of them. Daddo arrives, wheeling in Yiayia. She's so little but dressed as though she's about to promenade in the Plaka. Daddo sees me and blows a kiss. There is no sound from their end. Mum is looking frustrated. Just unmute it, Mum.

Sinead bounces in and bellows, 'Hello, Anna's family in Australia.' Everyone at the other end looks as though they've seen an apparition, with Mum adding a clear aura of, *What the*?

'Hello, hello,' answers Daddo. 'I love your brogue. From the west are you?' 'County Clare.'

Yiayia is squeezed in between Mum's and Daddo's chairs. Jimmi makes a theatrical entrance, pirouettes and says, 'Hi Anna's family. I'm Jimmi the Sami and Jimmi the Swede. Currently Jimmi the Greek. We danced and drank all night to celebrate Sinead's great Irish news.'

Thanks, Jimmi. No small talk just straight to the chase. 'And what was that then?' enquires Daddo.

'She can get married at home now, should she so want,' Jimmi says, laughing.

Daddo pauses briefly and then says, 'That's great for her then. My good friend Father Padraig might not think so, but he's not here. Lovely to meet you both.'

'So, introductions,' I say. 'Sinead and Jimmi, that's Jo, my mum, that's my wonderful yiayia in the middle and that's my fabulous daddo on the right.' I point at each of them in turn. I can see that Mum is not happy with my group approach to our Skype session.

She responds curtly, 'Greetings and may the God of Technology stay with us.'

'Goddess, maybe. Your daughter is a whizz with all things technical, Jo,' quips Jimmi. 'And with lots of other things too,' he adds.

That's enough from Jimmi. I move quickly and hold up the kangaroo and joey. 'Yiayia, you look beautiful and it's so good to see you. These two have seen all the same sights that I've seen. They loved dancing last night.'

Yiayia raises her left arm slowly and points at me. Everyone is silent. Mum fills the void. 'Anna, tell Yiayia about what you are doing and all about your friends.'

'Mum, we can all talk a bit about what we're doing and I'll let my friends tell you all about themselves.'

'Well, not all,' Jimmi says, chuckling.

Sinead chimes in, 'I'll start. We are all working on the Greek Financial Crisis.'

Very good Journalism 101, Sinead. Jimmi continues, 'Ani is passionate about how the crisis connects with the rest of the world, "*the bigger story*", as she calls it.'

'Mama loves big Greek stories, don't you?' Mum is looking at Yiayia who slowly nods.

Sinead fires up again. 'Ani wants each of us to find something that connects with us so we can, hopefully, make a documentary about something personal that connects us with Greece.'

Daddo asks, 'Sinead, do you have something in mind?'

'Well, it's a bit Irish, but I'm looking at links between Ireland and Greece.'

Daddo puts his arm around Yiayia's shoulders and says, 'This Ireland has been linked to this Greece for sixty years and I've often thought about things in common without ever finishing my list.'

'What's at the top of your list?' asks Sinead.

Yiayia turns slowly and gazes at Daddo who takes a deep breath before speaking. 'Well, they each have a rich history, full of wonderful stories and legendary characters and much of this is known by younger generations. Peia's love of Odysseus and his travels has certainly been passed on to Anna.'

'That's on my list too,' says Sinead, 'but if their greats could do amazing stuff then, why can't they pull something big out of the bag—gay marriage aside—now?' Nobody answers this question, which is promptly and independently categorised by all as a rhetorical question.

Before Mum even has a chance to fill the silence, Sinead continues. 'Number Two: they both have had their recent economic tiger moments and then plunged.' Sinead is on a roll. 'Number Three: their diaspora people return home during the booms and leave in the troughs.'

Yiayia smiles at the word '*diaspora*'. 'I think Mama likes that word,' Mum interjects. 'So does Ani,' we all chant in unison, followed by, 'Jinx!'

As the moment subsides, I say, 'Yiayia, we always celebrate Greek Independence Day but it's a funny sort of independence with strings attached.' I can see that Yiayia is with me so I continue. 'Greece only got its independence because it suited the world to sink the Turkish fleet.' God, that's a big statement from a girl with a very sore head who had no sleep. Yiayia is moving her lips, so I shut up. She's trying to say something. Her face is scrunching up. I almost can't bear to watch. Mum and Daddo are transfixed, watching her mouth as it opens and closes in exaggerated movements. No words come out. She moves her lips close to Daddo's ear and seems to be whispering something. I can see him trying to figure it out. They whisper to each other.

'Ah,' says Daddo. 'Yes, yes. Byron. That's Lord Byron.'

Yiayia has said 'Byron'. I'm amazed. 'Yes, Yiayia. Yes. Lord Byron. He was in favour of Greek independence.' I hope I don't sound condescending.

'Mad, bad and dangerous to know,' booms Jimmi. 'My sort of guy. I think he would have had fun on our mega celebration last night.' Yiayia listens as Jimmi continues. 'But he's one of the many British who have known what's best for Greece and what's best for Greece has always been what's best for the British.'

'They've also always known what's best for Ireland and that has always been what's best for the British,' Daddo adds. He claps his hands in enthusiasm. 'My friend Padraig would love to be part of this conversation.'

Jimmi launches off again. 'Sinead, I think we can say Number Four is that Ireland and Greece both hate the British with a passion. What do you think about that, Daddo? Can I call you Daddo?'

'Yes and yes,' Daddo agrees, nodding.

Now Jimmi is on a roll. 'I was over on one of the islands last week, talking and drinking and dancing with a lot of young English people, who just didn't seem to get why the Greeks don't really like to get too close to them. Kind of crazy of them to go to an island to party hard for a few days and expect to form deep and abiding friendships, but they were still perplexed.'

Sinead says, 'Number Five: they have both had bitter civil wars.' Not now, Sinead, not today. I haven't yet told Sinead about Teo. She continues, 'My great-grandfather died in the Irish Civil War.' At least she's switched it back to the Irish. Daddo moves his left hand into Yiayia's right one and places his free hand on top. Sinead continues, 'Number Six: holding grudges. At the time of my great-grandfather's death, in 1922 in Ireland, the Greeks were trying to reclaim Istanbul, which they lost in 1453. Is that, or is that not, a long time to hold a grudge?' She's headed back to the Greeks.

Yiayia is whispering to Daddo again. Her right hand is tight in both his hands. Daddo speaks.

'She says, *rembetika*.' Yiayia's done it again. Rembetika. Mum explains, even though there's no need. 'Blues music.'

Daddo adds, 'Yiayia loves it. Comes from when the Greeks didn't reclaim Istanbul.'

Both rooms are silent, as Yiayia looks me straight in the eyes, just as my previous night's excesses really begin to kick in. I'm about to suggest we say goodbye when she opens her mouth and out comes a sigh. Then there is no one else. Just her and me. 'Eyesore,' she says and shakes her head in frustration. 'Troy.' She breathes deeply. 'Ryots.' I want her to stop so I don't have to see and hear this. 'Tyros.' Her shoulders are heaving and every ounce of energy is being funnelled into her mouth. 'So. Try.' She shuts her eyes. So, try what? I wonder. 'Story. Teo.' She opens her eyes and nods straight at me. And then she starts sobbing. And Daddo is cradling her. And Mum is cradling Daddo. And I am so far away.

Jo

Mama is sleeping. Fitfully. Teo was her younger brother. He is presumed dead. Something happened when she was about fifteen, before she came to Australia. *Something*.

Padraig, the pacifist, took Da to Mass this morning. Padraig who believes in a life hereafter, in his dear land across the Irish sea. I envy his belief in one place that will be his home henceforth. He has nailed his Ithaca. I outsourced Da so I could spend some alone time with Mama in the calm of the morning. Technically, I am the adult in this epic medical drama, but I am an angry adult. Angry with both my parents. I feel teenage infuriation tinged with irritation, exasperation and antagonism. I would love to leave, just like my daughter.

I thought I knew most of the mama puzzle. I did not understand it, but I thought I knew it. I figured that I had come to terms with it as much as any of us come to terms with the odyssey that is pitched at us.

Maysa comes in and starts reading Mama's notes. 'She's not sleeping well at night,' she says. We have that in common. I would love to be able to kiss her. To hug her. To soothe her. Just like other mothers and daughters do instinctively, spontaneously, impulsively.

Oh, we can't kiss on a Monday,
A Monday would be so very good.

And we can't kiss on a Tuesday,
A Tuesday, I really wish we could.

Maysa looks up. 'The overnight nurse reported some new words: "mountains", "children", "walking", "blood" and "Frankie"?'

'Frankie was Da's sister.'

At my birth the top of my head popped out and in. I wasn't sure about coming out. And for much of my life, I was not certain about staying out. Until Anna. My grandmother fell in love with me instantly and the birth team spat on me three times to cast out the evil eye. Then my mother started bleeding. It could not be stemmed. It kept flowing. Post-partum. Then the ambulance. Then the hospital. Then the foggy days. Then a maternal death statistic.

A vibrant young woman who had had a love affair with a married Catholic man in Australia in 1960. Apparently, he loved my arty mother but would not, or could not, leave his wife and family. Too much shame associated with that. So, the young woman and her mother were planning to rear the child. But then a baby lost her mother, and the young woman's mother lost her only daughter and had a breakdown. So, the young woman's brother and his wife adopted Josephine Anna the Second. Then a baby who did not want to come out anyway had a new mother.

'Frankie. Da's sister,' I repeat. 'My other mother.'

Peia

'Our children will only remember war.' Mama is talking softly to Theía Trenna. Teo and Adelphos sit on the floor in the corner spellbound by a wooden puzzle. The women are slumped, exhausted by another icy day in the fields. Our meals are more and more meagre, as any 'spare' food goes to the frontline. I listen from the kitchen and fret about how I will stretch the food we have to fill the bowls. I ate earlier with the boys. I think that Mama has forgotten I'm here. The boys bound in and sniff their mothers' bowls of soup. I bribe them, like I would two puppies, with old biscuits and direct them upstairs. I want to listen to the women. Mama, speaking more loudly now, says 'They will never go to school.'

'The village school will reopen when it's over,' asserts Theía Trenna.

Mama counters, 'There will be no "Over". No village. Families, what's left of them, are evacuating. Many are heading north on foot. Your own sister has left.'

Theía Trenna replies, 'My sister has gone south because her husband was conscripted to the national army and she doesn't trust her chances here with us. I wish she hadn't gone but she's my sister and she'll probably be safer out of here.'

They stop talking as I carry in their soup and bread, placing them on the table by the kitchen. They thank me as they move wearily towards the table but don't ask me to join them, as they often do. 'I'll check the boys,' I say as I exit, but with no intention of doing so while their conversation continues. I quietly move some plates around the kitchen benches.

'So, our men are either fighting for one side or the other, reluctantly or not, or in prison or dead,' announces Mama.

'I still don't understand why anyone would leave their home for the mountains in the north. Why would you decide to live in a cave?' asks Theía Trenna.

Mama replies quickly, 'Because of the hunger, bombings, burnt villages, stolen livestock and, worst of all, the prospect of life after defeat.'

'They are short-term thinkers and you are tired,' answers Theía Trenna.

Mama replies, 'Yes to both, but my short-term thinking is going towards how I could help more. We should all be doing that.'

'We are helping by our work here. Growing food,' Theía Trenna says.

'Anyone can do that,' Mama explodes. 'We have been at war for so long now and with that defeat last December, we've started going backwards. We can't give up. We need people to fight for a free Greece.'

There is a pause and then Theía Trenna speaks, 'We are mothers. We can't fight. We have children who depend on us.'

Mama is on a run. 'Yes. They depend on us and they could be killed by us staying here. The national army is circling. The farm will be taken. We will all be taken. And I would rather fight for a free Greece than be forced by the national army to clear mines. I don't care what I do to help, but I'd like to do what I know I should do rather than just planting seeds. There is talk of enlisting more women and sending children north for a while so they can escape the bombs, have proper meals and go to school.'

I hear Mama's last sentence as the boys thump down the stairs, lurch towards their mothers and promptly stop the conversation.

Anna

After another all-nighter, Jimmi, Sinead and I find ourselves standing at a long bar in Dublin, Athens. We are surrounded by shiny bottles and dark wood. Last night, we celebrated Jimmi's birthday in various locations throughout the city. Now, hungry and unable to find a definitive Sami-Swedish breakfast, we are ordering Irish Breakfasts. Not the tea. The breakfast.

My eyes wander around the walls of the pub. I wonder what Yiayia would make of it and of us now. We are clad in our Eurovision Song Contest support outfits. I still feel guilty that I didn't put more effort into my Guy Sebastian look; I did manage to find his signature trilby, which looks a little flat now after its night on the town, a snappy waistcoat and a eucalypt boutonnière. There are so many homesickness-inducing eucalypt trees in Greece. Part of my remorse stems from the fact that Yiayia loves Guy. Not his romantic songs so much, but his soul stuff. She says, it's almost rembetika. She is sure he has Greek in his blood (as well as Malay, Indian, Sri Lankan, Portuguese and English).

Jimmi is wearing a blue suit and bright yellow T-shirt and has topped off his outfit with a huge red pompom hat that ties under the chin. He looks like a tea cosy but says that the bobble is his inner, now outer, Sami. He is gloating big time. A victorious Swede. His boy won. Ours came in a bloody good fifth.

Sinead's red carnation tattoo is surrounded by Celtic symbols.

Ireland didn't make the final cut. She claims that Ireland was robbed and because the Swedish winner has made so many anti-gay comments, she decided she needed to fly the flag for Ireland and gays. Well, not so much the flag really, but intricate hand drawings of androgynous leprechauns, knotty black crosses, viny green harps and a vivid rainbow.

We move to the garden and sit under our vines. A pondering Sinead asks, 'I wonder if my daideó ever came to this pub?' She's clearly more pissed than I thought. We are due in the office this afternoon with Ani. I can't have Sinead in banshee country.

'Maybe he was here in his dreams?' Jimmi suggests. 'Though I think even this place might be a bit young for your grandfather's dreams.'

'Your grandfather? Your daddo?' I query.

'My daideó. He fought in Greece in World War Two.'

Late-breaking news, Sinead. Through my haze of history in a very foggy head I'm sure that Ireland was neutral in World War Two. 'A coffee with your food?' I suggest to her. 'I'll order you one?'

'Never coffee with breakfast, always after,' she asserts. 'However, you can have beer with breakfast.'

'What self-respecting Irish man would have fought in World War Two?' Jimmi asks.

'At least 40,000 self-respecting Irish men volunteered to fight alongside the British,' Sinead answers back.

Piles of pork sausages and bacon appear. My food craving is about to be sated. We didn't just order meat, our meal is nicely balanced with black and white puddings, mushrooms, tomatoes, fried eggs, baked beans and hash. The vegetable kind. We eat. As Jimmi's food begins to kick in, he asks, 'So, what about my Skype List Number Four: Ireland and Greece both hate the British with a passion.'

'That list might just be a bit too simplistic, my dear Jimmi.

Why did any young man sign up for the war? Excitement, travel, work, money, family tradition, anti-fascism?' With some food in her, Sinead seems well on the road to recovery too.

'This black pudding is not as good as the one Mum makes. It needs some beers,' announces Jimmi, before he wanders off.

The garden wall advertises this as 'a place where there are only friends you haven't met'. Maybe it should add, 'whose stories you have yet to hear'. My food is kicking in too and my inner-Ani rises a little. 'What was your daddo doing in Greece then?' I ask Sinead.

Sinead scoops fried egg and baked beans into her mouth. 'My daideó was helping the British help the Greeks get rid of the Germans. He built things.'

'What sorts of things?'

'Airfields, roads, water lines and bridges. He loved literature but studied engineering. Never finished though.'

Jimmi returns with some very dark, very cold beers. I continue quizzing Sinead. 'How long have you known this?'

'About as long as you've known about your yiayia's brother being here somewhere.' Touché, Sinead. 'I was telling my ma on Skype about your Teo and she started weeping. She's not the weeping kind. Then she told me more than I knew about her da—my daideó. I didn't know he'd served. Let alone that he'd served in Greece. Apparently, it was a matter of shame for my mother's family at the time.'

'Here's to pink pork, darker beers and deeper stories,' announces Jimmi. It's hard to take him seriously with a big pompom bouncing on the top of his head.

Sinead takes a gulp of her beer but doesn't miss a beat. 'After the war, he was shunned and never able to finish his studies when he returned to Ireland or to get anything approaching an engineering job. Between tears, Ma said that he was a much-diminished man when he returned because of his experiences;

even more so when he couldn't get work in his profession at home. Might explain my unreasonable fascination with Greece.'

'I wonder where mine comes from?' contemplates Jimmi. His cutlery hovers between the black and white puddings. As though magnetically pulled, his cutlery abandons both in favour of the hash. Sinead continues, 'My ma studied literature and teaches it to truculent teenagers. She was inspired by her da's love of the old stories, the epics—his sole solace, as he was rejected by his own people. Apparently, he loved *Ulysses* the most. Both the original and the more modern Irish one.' Jimmi presses his deliberation button a little more and says, 'The epics aren't my main pub trivia expertise, but isn't Sinead's daideó's *Ulysses* the Roman name for Anna's yiayia's *Odysseus*?' I nod. 'I must read them. I must read everything ever written. I'd set myself my birthday as the day I'd have my Ani-story sorted. It hasn't happened. But you two each have something pretty interesting to dig for.'

He's sounding less victorious and more mournful, so I swing back to Sinead. 'What's your plan then, Sinead?'

'Back to journalism basics, I reckon. Why was my daideó here? Who was he with? When? Where? And why did telling me about him make my ma weep so? And your plan, Anna?'

'Finding Teo, I guess.'

Sinead asks, 'What's your plan, Jimmi? Other than reading every book ever written?'

'First, I guess to answer my parents' messages wishing me Happy Birthday. I haven't spoken to them since I've been here and they phoned me several times yesterday. They weren't too thrilled about me coming here; they see it as another addition to my long list of life distractions.'

I lift my glass and propose a toast, 'Here's to distractions then.' Ani appears with a Swedish scarf wrapped around her neck, carrying a parcel wrapped in red, blue, green and yellow.

'Jimmi, Happy Birthday! *Hronia Pola*!' she bellows as a waiter appears with more beers and a bottle of ouzo.

Jimmi's pompom disappears somewhere near Ani's breasts while he simultaneously cries at the parcel. 'Sami colours, Sami colours,' he repeats. There goes my assumption that the green and yellow might be in deference to me.

'Open your present, Jimmi,' Sinead urges.

'The wrapping is too beautiful to destroy,' he says wiping his eyes. And I had always thought it was the Irish who topped the world in the sentimentality stakes. 'How did you know we were here?' he asks Ani.

'When you are not at work or on location, you are mostly here,' Ani replies, pouring some ouzo into the glasses.

Jimmi begins picking very precisely at the parcel's tape. Then we see that it is a series of parcels. The first parcel contains, what looks like, salted fish. Jimmi beams. The second parcel looks like sausages and some sort of meat. He says, 'Surely not! Is this what I think it is?'

Ani replies, 'And what might you be thinking?' 'Reindeer?'

'Cured reindeer,' Ani confirms. 'We don't have a shipping line for nothing.'

Jimmi carefully opens the next package. He looks wide-eyed at Ani. 'Yes, reindeer cheese.' He's speeding up a bit. The inner- and outer-Sami seems very happy. The parcel produces a pita-like bread. 'Glödkaka,' he yells. 'Nothing personal, Ani, but we do this better than the Greeks.' We all drink to that. He then opens a punnet of little berries. Like blueberries but orange. 'Cloudberries! Cloudberries,' he exclaims. Next comes a black pudding. 'Ani, ours is, of course, the best black pudding in the world. You are very clever.' We drink to that too.

Ani announces that she must leave. 'Maybe we should all have a day off?' she suggests. 'There's nothing super urgent at the office.' I feel momentarily guilty about all my impersonations of her. 'But Jimmi, you have one job today. Ring your parents. *Hronia Pola.*' She exits stage left.

Jo

I am with Maysa in the staff cafeteria. Apparently the coffee is better here; however, while I may have been upgraded to business class, I am experiencing no superior caffeine benefits so far. Maysa is explaining the family-centred care model for stroke patients. 'We see the stroke patients and the family as a unit,' she says. She has misdiagnosed our family. We are more a Peia Peaked Model. 'Collaboration and partnership are very important.' She will get that from everyone except the patient. 'The best results come if we all work together,' she adds, as she nibbles away at a dun-coloured vegan cake while I scatter rich chocolate flakes around me.

'Could we take a step back?' I ask, as I retrieve some flakes from the table. 'Of course.'

'Mama did not recognise me. There is obviously significant memory loss.'

She toys with an almost dead bit of cake. 'Peia's ability to express ideas and thoughts has been dislocated. Patients have difficulty with words and sometimes memories of people—it often comes and goes—but other knowledge can endure pretty well. It looks, at this stage, like she is one of those patients.' I tentatively sip at my lukewarm coffee as she continues, 'From what we can tell, her intellectual functions seem good. She is smart. Where did she attend school?'

'Because of the war, Mama was pretty much home-schooled by her mama, who had attended school.'

'And her father?'

'Similar. Because of war, he was often away from their home. But he was a farmer.' 'So, both her parents were articulate? And spoke good English?'

'Yes. Her father learned English from mixing with other soldiers and her mother from her schooling.'

'So, she came from a home of words.' 'And love,' I add.

My comment provokes a direct look from Maysa. 'I might get another cake. Anything for you?' she asks.

'Just water, please.' She returns with a carafe of water and a replica of her first cake. 'I love these.' She pauses and eats a little. 'When you were growing up, what was your home like?'

'I came from a home of drip-fed secrets. I thought I knew about, and had accepted as much as I could, the secrets that mattered. But Mama having a younger brother is a lot to take in right now. It could explain so much about then. But now Mama does not always recognise me. So, currently I cannot see love and she cannot say words.'

'That is, in part, why family collaboration and partnership are so important to her recovery. Harry talked to me about her very first years in Australia. I am not breaking any confidences to say that she arrived here with some big burdens. It seems as though he, Theío Angel, Frankie and Móraí Josephine were all part of Peia's support network in different ways. He said that he hasn't talked to you much about the pre-you period but I hope he does when he feels ready to.'

'When he feels ready to? He has already had five or so decades to do so.' 'I hope he will yet. Where did Peia work when you were a child?'

'For a union.' Talking about Mama chokes me up. She was great in the workplace. She saved many of her current friends from dire situations. I am sure it is where she earned the bonus loyalty points that she is still reaping. 'My other mother, Frankie,

Da's sister, was a dress designer at a clothing factory. She initially got Mama a job there.' I pause and take a breath.

Talking about my other mother also chokes me up. 'Frankie was also in the union so, out of hours, Mama often tagged along with her and Móraí Josephine to all sorts of interesting events.' Maysa ponders another bit of brown cake. 'Mama got the bug, proved to be a great workplace negotiator and had plenty to work with. There were high numbers of female migrants in the manufacturing industry and really high numbers in the clothing industry, which was not, at the time, known for its fair wages or good working conditions.'

'Yes, I know, it was not that great when my mother was a clothing worker either,' Maysa says.

'As Frankie was doing really well as a designer, it suited her for Mama to pick up the union mantle. Like Mama, most of the women had never been in paid work before and many were juggling their Australian experiences with no formal child care arrangements and most were much less schooled and skilled than she was in English.'

'And Móraí Josephine, with her experience, was also very important for your mother at that time.'

'Yes, she told me that she was often the instigator of their evenings out. Frankie and Mama would come home tired and not want to move. But she would convince them to dress up—often in Frankie's 1950s creations—and go places, like the conservatorium to hear women speaking on employment rights and equal pay and, heaven forbid, on the rights of married women to work for equal pay. Or on weekends, they would all go to the exhibitions of the top female artists, which Frankie, in particular, loved and was inspired by.'

'A little inspiration is exactly what Peia needs for both functional improvement and neurological renewal,' Maysa says.

'Mama is usually her own inspiration. I don't think she's

convinced about making the effort. I read that aphasia can just go away.' I wonder if Maysa hears that hope from every family.

She is being buzzed. 'Sorry, I have to go. We want to try Peia with a home-based rehabilitation program. I still need to convince her doctor. I know you are sceptical. I am a little too. But I think home might set her up for a better recovery.'

After she leaves, I sit toying with the last of my chocolate crumbs.

Peia

Word of mouth has lured everyone in. The priest is looking tense and not scattering any blessings. We could do with some. Teo and Adelphos are excited to see other children and start playing with them near the trees in the dark square. A tired-looking commander, revolver astride his hip, is standing on a bench. Below stands an equally tired-looking Vaska. The commander is thanking everyone for their work so far. 'So far,' says Theía Trenna, 'it's been our children's whole lives.' A murmur of agreement.

'We are all playing our part in the fight for Greece's freedom,' the commander continues. I wish I could fly away because, while I like the talk of freedom, I know that we aren't here to hear that democracy has trumped the dictators. The commander continues, 'The King has friends in very high places. Our enemies have their prey in their sights and are beginning to fight back on a bigger scale. But we cannot stop this freedom fight. There is too much at stake.' He may be expecting applause, but none is forthcoming. He continues, 'Soon this village will be too dangerous for children. Many children have already been killed. There will be more bombs, napalm bombs, provided by our former allies and dropped on you and your children for the King by the Greek Army.'

The heavy weight of his words fills the hall, Mama speaks, 'The same allies we fed, and fought alongside, against fascism.'

The commander speaks again, 'There are some decisions to be made. We need to fight from the mountains. The King's army is days away. You will be killed, imprisoned or conscripted.'

'How will it be safe for the children in the mountains?' the priest asks.

'Our allies to the north will provide safe havens for the children until the war is over. We just need to get the children away for a while.'

'How will the children travel out of Greece safely?' Mama asks.

The commander replies, 'We will help with the transportation.'

'And their mothers will accompany them?' Mama asks.

'The older children will look after the younger children,' he answers.

Mama's arms squeeze more tightly around my shoulders. She cuts to the chase. 'You mean the older girls will look after the children?'

Vaska, the soldier, looks directly at me as the commander speaks, 'Some soldiers will also accompany the children.'

A woman speaks, 'My job is my children. I need to be with them.' Others murmur in agreement.

The commander continues, 'This is just for a little while. We need everyone who can to fight against our enemies. Mothers will be together again with children in a free democracy after our glorious victory.' The message is sinking in around the room. Groups of people begin to talk to each other. The church whitewashers are working their worry beads. 'We need to prepare on a new scale and must have more soldiers. We are significantly outnumbered. We do not want partisans to be captured by the King's army when they could be aiding a victory.'

I want to be under my pile of acorns in the forest listening to the boys playing or dancing in our small green valley in summer with both my parents. It's been so long since I've seen Papa. The walls breathe deeply. From behind me, Mama places her hands on my shoulders and kisses the back of my neck. I know what she wants to do and what she wants me to do. She will be missing from me.

Anna

More than 50,000 people died in the Greek Civil War.

More statistics. A night and early morning immersed in learning what I didn't know about the Greek Civil War, which was almost nothing. If I'm lucky, so far I have located about one per cent of what I might need to 'find' Teo. I'm also thinking about what's been happening in Greece since I arrived.

During the Greek Civil War, more than 500,000 Greeks were displaced from their homes.

How do you find someone in a country that was ravaged by war last century? I can hardly get past the stark black-and-white photographs.

Mass graves. Desperate faces in a line behind barbed wire fences.

Greece has just delayed its 300-million-euro debt repayment to the International Monetary Fund. That means that 1.5-billion euros will now be owing at the end of the month. Last week, we walked through a rubbish-piled university, past the anti-IMF graffiti, to hear the Prime Minister caution the international community against imposing humiliating stipulations on his country. More photos.

Dead bodies lying in Syntagma Square. British tanks?

The Prime Minister has described the debt plan as the strangulation of a country; a bad moment for Europe; a matter of moral order against the founding principles of Europe. Others in parliament are calling it blackmail and the talk of a snap election continues.

Strangulated corpses hanging from trees.

This weekend Sinead and I were going to work together on our Ani-stories but in the midst of this tumultuous political time, she has found love, lust or at least a distraction.

Beautiful women carrying rifles.

Jimmi has headed to an island for some soul searching (also known as beer searching).

Men, women and children, huddled and hungry.

When Yiayia was six, the Italians invaded Greece. The Greeks pushed them back, but it was not long before the Germans arrived. While the Greek Government and the King bolted to Egypt, resistance to the invasion was provided by EAM-ELAS (communist-controlled) and the EDES (the Greek Democratic National Army).

When I was six, clever little me used to recite precociously, 'But now I am six, I'm as clever as clever, So I think I'll be six now for ever and ever.'

Yiayia would not have wanted to be six for ever and ever.

When I was ten, I was occupied with my Tamagotchi. A digital toy to feed and nourish.

When Yiayia was ten, she faced occupation and famine and soon thereafter the Civil War started.

Holding worry beads with a kangaroo and a joey doesn't stop my feelings of ignorance, loneliness and homesickness.

Children carrying banners.

The British, still at war with Germany, armed Nazi collaborators to help them act against the demonstrators who were supporting the resistance movement (a movement with which the British had previously been allied). In Athens, twenty-eight civilians, mostly young children, were killed and hundreds injured.

During the Greek Civil War more than 24,000 Greek children crossed its northern borders. Australia, with other countries, worked to reunite children with their immediate and extended families.

Australia did that? Mum said that Yiayia had been talking in her sleep about "mountains", "children" and "walking".

By the end of November 1950, 172 unaccompanied children had arrived in Australia.

Skype buzzes. It's very late here, but morning in Australia. I answer, 'Hello, Theo.'

'How are you?'

'Sad and lonely,' I announce. He certainly brings out the blurter in me. 'Are you okay?' he asks. He does that bit very well though.

'Yes, I'm okay, but home alone in Athens on a Saturday night; well, Sunday morning now. My friends have abandoned me.'

'Your *other* friends?'

'Okay, my *other* friends.' He's still sexy, even on a slightly blurry Skype screen. And I think he's in bed. 'Sleeping in today?' I ask.

'Yes, it was a bit of a late one. A few beers after a footy match led to a party at someone's house where there was a makeshift band and sometime during the night I became the lead singer and guitarist.'

What can't this boy do? 'I didn't know you sang or played guitar.'

'I was in a band in Greece with that mate who died on the building site. Last night was the first time I've had a go since. Beer courage.'

'Go you.'

'Not much sleep but I had a really good time. My sources tell me that you haven't spent many Saturday nights home alone in Athens.'

'True enough. This was a particularly quiet one.'

'I didn't think you'd answer. But the rain woke me and I thought of you.'

'Do you only associate me with rain?'

'No, but you sound as though you might need a hug. A hug-hug, of course.' The eyebrows are lined up and he's wearing that winning smile that charms young and old alike.

'Your hugs can get a bit complicated.' '*My* hugs?'

'Okay, *our* hugs.' Time to change the subject. 'What music did you play last night?'

'It was a bit different to what we had at your yiayia's Community Club. But people did want me to play "*Greek Stuff*".'

'Your fans?'

'My midnight fans, who might not remember me today.' 'What's "*Greek Stuff*" at midnight?'

'Some were chanting "*Zorba, Zorba, Zorba, Zorba*". I told them that I had left my bouzouki in Athens, but improvised some Greek-ish stuff on guitar.'

'Chick magnet?' Where the hell did that come from? 'What?'

'Girls, women—did they throw themselves at you?'

'I know what a "chick magnet" is, thanks. No. Proper Aussie blokes keep their chicks on a leash.'

'And proper Greek blokes don't?' Yiayia can't get her words out and I can't keep my words in. '"Zorba, Zorba, Zorba, Zorba". Play me something?'

'I don't have a guitar here. I could sing you something?'

I'd never had a sexy young man sing to me before. I wait, listening.

Something woke me up, Must have been the rain.

His voice is very deep.

And for no good reason here you are, Inside my head again.

Deeper on another level.

I know I won't go back to sleep now,

I'm in a mood.

Must be the midnight rain, the midnight rain.

Now an almighty coughing fit. 'Do you want me to get you some water?' I ask.

'Yes.' A bit less coughing. 'Please. Too many cigarettes last night.'

'You haven't given them up yet then?' 'You?'

'I haven't quite stopped completely yet. And I had a hard time yesterday.' 'Hard? How?'

'I suppose more like depressing. I've started on Yiayia's mission and realised how little I know about her life here. Finding Teo will be as hard as finding Adriana's treasure. She's another of Yiayia's female pirate icons.'

'Do you need a cigarette?' 'Need and want.'

'I could join you; just to be polite.'

What a champion. 'I'll need to go outside.'

'Me too.' As we each move to our balconies, he says, 'Tell me about Adriana? Sing the story if you like.'

'I'll leave the singing to you, but interestingly she almost has the same name as my boss, Ani.' Outside it is dark and warm. 'The story goes that she stole a ship full of sapphires and gold in the Aegean, stayed with the treasure and sent her pirates ashore to find food and wine for a celebration.'

'That bit is very Greek,' he says, as he puffs on his cigarette.

I can hear the Australian rain. 'The pirates arrived at an island church where the locals were celebrating a feast day.'

'That too is very Greek and could be any day of the year,' he says, laughing.

I notice that there is no pyjama top in sight, only his lovely hairy chest. I wonder if he's cold. 'The pirates joined in the dancing and started singing a strange entrancing song.'

'That's very siren-like,' he says. 'A bit like you.'

I ignore his comment, inhale and continue, 'The locals were mesmerised by the song and the pirates were just about to kill them and steal their food, wine and church embellishments when the Virgin Mary appeared.'

'Very timely that one. She stopped the impending disaster?'

'Well, no. Just reversed it. The locals then slaughtered all the pirates with the Virgin's blessing.'

'And did Adriana come and take on the Virgin?'

'Not that either. When the pirates didn't return, she found a very secret place for the treasure, sat down in satisfaction on a clifftop—maybe with a cigarette—and then tragically fell into the sea. Some versions claim it was suicide. The treasure is still hidden somewhere.'

'I could come over and help you find it.' 'I thought you were never coming back?'

'It's my mother's sixtieth later this year. My parents are trying to bribe me with an airfare. I'm thinking about it.'

I see an eyebrow rise and say, 'Doesn't sound like you're very committed to your Greek scorched earth policy?'

'I could travel with your mum. Keep her company on the flight.'

'You can look her in the eye now, can you?'

'We get along okay. Your yiayia doesn't cut her much slack.'

'Mum's still not sure if she'll be able to come. It depends on how Yiayia goes with the next bit, now that she's being expelled from the hospital.' His song is ear-worming me.

'And last night I got to thinking about my mate who died. I could come for his anniversary.'

That's very Greek. We slowly and simultaneously stub out our cigarettes. The airwaves, which are now agreeably silent, are interrupted by the ear-splitting buzzing of the persistent inside intercom. *Bugger.* Probably a keyless Sinead returning full of love with her mate. *Double bugger.* I am not inclined to move.

'You'd better see who needs you so urgently,' he says. 'Call me next time?'

Jo

It's my first morning back at work. I head downstairs to my basement office with its slim street level window that lets in some natural light. I am happy to be back in a world in which I am good.

For the last couple of months, I have subcontracted my contracts, keeping an eye on things, but definitely not working much on my business. I have always had a steady stream of design work, even when Anna was little. If I stuck to what I knew I was good at, we were just fine.

What is not so fine is that this week Mama has headed from hospital to home. Home is next door, on the other side of my office wall. Unfortunately, she did not pass the hospital's test with flying colours. Her official report card would probably read something along the lines of, 'While Peia had some moments of utter brilliance, a much more consistent positive approach, aligned with more personal effort, would, in all likelihood, position her and her family for a much better future'. She even alienated fellow stroke sufferers and I don't imagine that the staff were lining up to work with her. Some words, which were never expressed out loud by those she met, might include, 'Rude, truculent, detached, self-absorbed, stubborn and erratic'.

Calandra is her rostered home-rehabilitation buddy today, as Da is cleaning, clearing and tinkering with all Mama's new aids for the home-based rehabilitation phase. It is such a pity that they cannot swap roles at this stage. He has a much better temperament for being a patient. Their front porch now sports a ramp, supplied (apparently at a great rate) by one of Mama's young tradie contacts.

As if Da's new role is not enough, he has decided to clean out the back shed. It used to be Theío Angel's workshop but over the last few decades it has become the place where both houses store all the things that they did not want to throw out but did not want to keep inside.

I have promised that I will give Da a hand at lunchtime and that is now. He wants to make the shed a sort of conservatory so that Mama can sit close to her garden. Da is not short on imagination but can be dithery in execution. However, as I have a lot to catch up on in here, my plan is simply to take instruction and tip my cap as necessary.

I hear a shout downstairs from the back door. 'Jo, Jo, when are you coming to get your things?' This is a new angle; I'm fifty-five and he's only just now asking me to get my crap out of his shed. 'And Anna's things!' he yells.

'Da, it might be a bit early for her, but should we try and Skype Anna so she can point to what she wants to keep and what she wants to toss?' No reply from upstairs as my ironic question floats away.

The backyard is Berlin before the wall came down. This is not dithery Da. There are different zones of occupation. Da's zone is very compact. He has put his things in boxes near the potato garden. Spare parts for most of the original appliances in their home (formerly Móraí Josephine's home). Mama's pile is more free-flowing and borderless. It edges what were once this summer's tomato, zucchini, capsicum, eggplant and cucumber crop. Piles of books in Greek and English sit next to rich, hand-embroidered materials, which must never have been quite right for her imagined outfits. There is also a line of postal tubes within which there are probably bright screen prints, making strident calls for female workers to unite.

Laid out, on our side of where a dividing garden fence would be if it existed, are Anna's goods, packed in different suitcases with different logos from the different decades of her life. Most of my goods comprise large canvases. An outdoor art show under our winter grapevine. So many canvases and the one closest to me is signed with a great big 'V'. I honestly did not know it was in the shed. It's bold. Abstract. Strong.

'V' (also known as Romeo) was my first love in what became a Capulet and Montague scale war, instigated by my mama and happily perpetuated by his mother. The (official) reasons for why he and I were not allowed to be together remain unknown to me. It is unlikely that they will ever be known to me now. *Vasilios, Vasilios, why have you turned up now?*

'Da, why was one of Vasilios's canvases allowed to live in the shed for years, when he was not allowed in our home for even a minute?'

'I didn't notice a canvas of his in the shed.'

'It's here in front of me.'

'I didn't notice it in the shed.' This is how conversations go with Da sometimes. 'What next then, Da?'

'You take yours. I take ours. And we both gain a conservatory.' That bit still takes a lot of imagination, but I tip my metaphorical cap and follow my instructions.

Canvases. My start-stop world. I commence dusting and sorting them. Some of them should go. But some are so near completion and some are okay. Actually, some are pretty good for their time.

Parking Anna's bulging, closed suitcases in her old room is mostly straightforward. However, as I do so, one case bursts open, probably from the strain of all those draft words of hers being locked up and trapped close together for so long. And with the words, out bursts a little wooden pencil case. *Mine, mine, mine*! My daughter: the thief. Theío Angel made that for, and gave that to, a little round me. A dark wooden pencil case with a sliding top.

It does not slide open without some effort but, inside on top of some beautifully sharpened coloured pencils, is a carefully rolled fading sketch of a little girl under a cypress tree. Mama is that little girl. My canvases. Vasilios's canvas. I must get back to my work.

I pop out for a final check. Da has moved his pile somewhere and he and Padraig are sitting near the shed, in his previously occupied zone, having a beer in a patch of sunshine. Each one points regularly at the shed, gesticulating. Undoubtedly two of the world's best conservatory designers. Lucky Mama.

Da is smiling. 'Jo Jo, is this yours?' From his lap he produces a little handmade hoe. I think this is what happens when you never really leave home.

Peia

I'm back at home. They have given up on me becoming part of a hospital community of stroke survivors. Harry is out the back. Jo Jo is at work. I am briefly a community of one. It's hard to fathom if the noises in my head are an aphasia community or a memory community.

Dit, dit, dit, dit, dit, dit, ditter. Are the noises saying '*quitter*'?

When I was born, Greece was a republic. When I was one, the King came back.

Dit, dit, dit, dit, dit, dit, ditter. Are the noises daytime gunfire? Surely not here in Australia. Stay still. Dit, dit, dit, dit, dit, dit, ditter. Much louder. More guns? Much closer. Too close?

Theía Trenna and Mama have taken the boys to the field today to let the boys 'run off some steam'. She hasn't taken Teo there since Papa left last time. I should be looking out for them but I'm stuck on our balcony. A community of one.

Dit, dit, dit, dit, dit, dit, ditter. The noises are turning into a clatter. *Am I a quitter?*

When I was two, the King gave us a dictator. When I was five, the Italians came but the dictator said, 'No' to them. My parents helped pass messages through the mountains. Like magicians.

Dit, dit, dit, dit, dit, dit, ditter.

Block the noise out. No blue in the sky today. Just massed clouds. I'll fly out and check on the fields. I could check on Harry at the back and Jo Jo at work and see if she's smoking outside. Hard to catch a thermal today though. I just need to keep an even pace, save my energy and rise above the clouds.

When I was seven, the dictator died, the Germans came and the King ran away.

If I'm on the ground, I don't soar. Same bird but slower with my head stretched up, ever on alert. And when I'm really scared my head disappears right into my neck. That's the Quitter Bird.

When I was eight, Greece had a mountain government. It provided schooling and girls were allowed to attend the lessons.

Storks don't look like they are made for flying, but look at me. Not a quitter. No, no, no, no, no. Never.

A strong young body. Graceful, long, broad black-and-white wings (both sides working), an elegant unlined neck stretched forward and slim red catwalk legs trailing behind. All in unison. Just like in the dance.

There's a village meeting tonight. I want to go but I'll have to return to the ground.

On the ground, the Quitter Bird's nose is red; her feet are all webby; her eyes look bruised. Her neck transforms from elegant to scrawny. Her glorious ruff feathers are dank and clumpy.

When I was ten, the Germans left and we all went to Saloniki for a happy day of celebration; however, then the King returned and the British gave us the government we 'had to have for a while'.

The meeting is an update on the war from the local commander. An update on *this* war. When I was twelve, the government we 'had to have for a while' became the government 'we had to have'.

These storks have watched my life as I have watched theirs.

Now I am fourteen, I am lying on our balcony watching some white storks guarding our chimney. I wish I could scoop everyone I love into my bill and fly far away.

Dit, dit, dit, dit, dit, dit, ditter. Stork family clatter. Deafening sometimes, like ours.

Jo

'Mum. How are you?' It is Sunday morning in Athens and Anna is on time. The shoulders have changed to an even deeper brown. She must blend in even more now. Before I have a chance to answer, she asks, 'How is home-based rehabilitation going?'

'That might need a cigarette.' Since returning to work, I've allowed myself one a day. 'Thank you for being there. I was not going to let myself smoke alone.'

I do not want to start our Skype with home-based rehabilitation. I decide to change the subject to a more standard Sunday morning question, 'What did you get up to last night?'

'Home alone. Jimmi was away and Sinead was busy with a new "interest".' 'Do you like her new "interest"?'

'I don't really know. They both just speak in giggles and throw each other knowing looks when they are here. How's Yiayia?' She is in journalist mode.

'She is home. I deliberately stayed in my office most of the week. A roster of daytime buddies, organised by Maysa, has commenced. Its key members are Calandra, paired with other friends and Padraig and Theo, as available.'

'No Daddo?'

'As well as being my correspondent on the ground, or on the other side of the wall, Da is a locum from what I can work out. I have received some brief reports from him, but he and Padraig have been somewhat distracted by their collaboration on the

Grand Designs Project. I am expecting Kevin McCloud to turn up at some stage with a film crew.'

'And the project is?'

'Turning Theío Angel's shed into one of Australia's foremost conservatories; however, I think the episode will be highly suitable for a mass audience. Slightly eccentric non-professional builders. A bit of tension within the relationship. A survival story nearby. Deep personal history with the site. Iteratively changing the design during the project and a fluid budget.'

'Mum, don't hold back, will you? Have they not involved you in their conservatory vision?'

'The "they" on this occasion are Da and Padraig. A surprise for Mama. You know how she loves them? Not.'

'Interesting. Has the site been excavated yet?'

'Initial clearings produced: a canvas by an old boyfriend of mine and some packed suitcases of yours, containing evidence of a crime you committed against me.'

'Mum, you shouldn't be opening my suitcases.'

'One burst open in front of me, spewing forth a little wooden pencil case with a sliding top.' 'Just keeping it safe for you. Tell me about Canvas Boyfriend?'

'Perhaps, if I forgive you.'

'Was there something in the pencil case, other than your neat, coloured, sharp pencils?'

'A drawing of a little girl under a cypress tree.'

'Can you scan it for me?' Full Anna mode. No apologies. She continues.

'I've started trying to find Teo. The drawing may help, though I'm not sure how.'

'How are you finding time to find Teo while covering Greece's financial woes?'

'I look at my mostly-empty Teo folder in between the Finance Minister imploring the world not to humiliate Greece; the

German Chancellor pointing to the sand in the Greek hourglass not running on European time; share markets falling; and Greece warning that a deal is unlikely at the next round of talks.'

'Teo is stuck in your head?'

'Yes. He is now always there when something else isn't. And I don't even know what he looks like.'

'Is Theo stuck in your head at all?'

'Not stuck, but he's there because I can imagine what he looks like and he sometimes appears live on my screen. How is he going to find time for the buddy roster? He's getting a lot of work.'

'I think he can pick and choose a bit. And he likes her and she listens to him.'

'Mum, tell me all about Canvas Boyfriend.'

'Well, I have not forgiven you over the pencil case incident, but when I was in Year 12, we had an energetic and enlightened teacher at our school who arranged some extra drawing classes for us at the art school. Our parents did not know at the time that their daughters, safely sheltered from the world in an all girls' school, were greatly enjoying the pleasures of life drawing classes.'

'Mum that's fantastic!'

'So, in this teenage love story, Vasilios was a student at the art school and the studio assistant for our class. He encouraged me with my life drawings. One evening, during art school break, I went to class as usual but there was no class. We shared an easy and funny conversation, a two-dollar pizza (for which he paid) and our sketchbooks. He liked my life drawings and I liked his abstracts.'

'You lied to your parents about going to class.'

'And the next week too. I wanted to see if he was suitable to meet Mama and I thought he was going well. Criterion One: he was a Greek Boy. Criterion Two: his family came from the north of Greece. Criterion Three: he lived at home with his mother.

Criterion Four: he wanted to meet my family. Criterion Five: he was a very good kisser but did not seem in a rush to get me into bed—that last criterion was more for Mama than me.'

'So?'

'I did not know at the time but one of Mama's friends saw us in the restaurant. Within minutes the liaison was reported to Mama and by morning it was reported to the school and the art school.'

'What happened?'

'A big scene, when I got home. A bigger scene, the next day at school. Our brave teacher disappeared from our class and our school. There were no more life drawing classes. Vasilios got some sort of seventies art school talk about students and boundaries. We tried to keep a furtive-something going but it dissipated, ably fanned by our mother's winds in each of our homes.'

'So, I suppose you brought shame upon his home and he brought shame on yours?'

'That's what my teenage-self was told. But, as a result of the shed clean out, Da has put Canvas Boyfriend right in front of me now. Why?'

Peia

As I sit at my window in my hospital-approved home armchair, looking at the urban life below, Calandra clashes and sings in my kitchen. Sometimes it's her singing that is the loudest; other times it's her clashing. Both are sweet in the air today; the winds might be blowing me.

The day after the village meeting, Mama is at home but in another world. Teo is still asleep. She is staring at our cypress tree in our winter valley. 'Why have you declared another day off?' I ask.

'Another day off?' she responds.

'We had one during the last war when we made galaktoboureko and you gave me the kangaroos.' A faint smile appears.

Cacophonous Calandra. It's what she does when she pretends to cook. It means that she has procured an expensive tasty something from nearby. The louder the noise, the more delicious the treat.

And you can eat me on a Sunday, a Sunday, a Sunday,
'Cause that's no day to rest.

Mama sighs, 'I think we should make another one.' 'What about the fighters who need our food?' I ask.

'Both sides are having a day off today too. For the patron saint of galaktoboureko.' In the last war, I would have believed the story. Today, I am going with it.

'A new saint?' I ask.

'New times call for new saints,' she says.

'Why have you never told me about this saint?' I ask.

'Because the feast day occurs only when it is really needed. Not every year. Not even every other year. A saint for imaginative women.'

I move to the kitchen, calling back, 'So, imaginative woman, we will need milk and eggs and thin pastry.'

'Everything is thin at the moment.' She laughs at her comment. 'And butter?' I ask.

'We have permission to melt anything during the war.'

I want this game to go on forever. 'What about the smells from the oven?' I ask.

'What do you think?' she asks.

'We can inhale the smells if we imagine all the galaktoboureko ever made.'

'Of course.' She leads. 'Slowly now. One, two, three: inhale.' She draws me in to her arms and hugs me and then someone else is tugging our skirts. We lift Teo between us and he joins our hug. I am still looking at both of them and inhaling as Calandra comes towards me singing to a galaktoboureko.

Oh, we can eat it on a Monday,
A Monday, a Monday is very, very good.

And we can eat it on a Tuesday,
A Tuesday, a Tuesday, in fact I wish we could.

She pauses. I want to join in with her singing. But while the words are in my head, they remain stuck inside. They refuse to travel. To migrate beyond my lips. To go where they should. They are the quitters. I am not the quitter here. Not today.

However, today, for the first time, behind the quitter words, there they are. I can see them now as clearly as I can see Calandra.

After nights of walking and searching, just inside a cave, at the top of a bed of acorns, a kangaroo and a joey. Placed not dropped. They want to be found.

In her full frock, Calandra twirls on her toes with the plate balanced in her hand. It's definitely a procuring frock not a cooking frock. 'Almost perfect. Too many years in the hospitality industry,' she contends. Calandra is a specialist in a particular part of the hospitality industry. I first met her through my union work; she was not a member of any recognised union at the time. 'Let's do this, Peia.' Do what? I wonder. She sighs and places the cake on the dining table. 'I'm not convinced that the team at your hospital found the way from your head to your heart.'

I don't blame the hospital. There has just been no room for anything in my head since Teo came back. He seems to be the one blocking the road to my heart. 'I can sing you back and you can dance you back.' Is she trying to make me dance for her supper? Is the procuring frock about procuring my heart?

'Don't look so worried. We've done bigger things in our time than a little singing and dancing.' She is squatting down in front of me, blocking my view of the cake. Our eyes are at level, she places my arms around her neck and her arms under my arms and around my back. 'Slowly now. One, two, three: Stand.' We must look like an old couple on the last dance of the night. Tragedy and comedy. She starts singing.

Oh, you can kiss me on a Monday,
A Monday, a Monday is very, very good.

She's swaying me the tiniest little bit.

Or you can kiss me on a Tuesday,
A Tuesday, a Tuesday, in fact I wish you would.

I'm swaying me the tiniest little bit. Some of my joints have joined.

Or you can kiss me on a Wednesday,
A Thursday, a Friday and Saturday is best.

We are both swaying now and each move one little step to each side. My mind has joined my body. I can see the cake.

But never, never on a Sunday, a Sunday, a Sunday,
'Cause that's my day of rest.

My knees are with me. My lower back is part of my upper back. 'Gain,' I say.

'Yes,' she yells. 'A gain!'

'Again?' I ask.

'Yes, yes! A gain, again!'

We do it again and again, each time with a bit more confidence. Then she helps me lower myself back into my chair. My urban street is still in the same place but it has a little wind in it. She twirls to the table and then with a full flourish presents me with the best ever (procured) galaktoboureko.

Dance heals.

Anna

Jimmi is with Ani, speaking with some of her contacts on the islands about the increasing number of refugee arrivals. It's been a mad month, starting with a strong earthquake that was felt in Athens. On this rare morning, Sinead is at home by herself and neither of us need (or want) to be anywhere else soon. We are having a slow start together. I am brewing her tea and she is making my coffee.

As I turn the teapot, I eye the strainer and cosy and declare, 'Well, we wanted to cover interesting stories.' In the last weeks, her friend has been around less at home and at work while we've had emergency summits, deals and no-deals, counter-offers, bailouts, reduced bailouts and no bailouts, closed banks, a referendum announcement and a missed deadline for a billion-dollar loan repayment.

'So many stories,' she replies. 'I'm still foggy about how we'll weave all our threads together coherently. That's the problem with only Ani seeing the big story and how it should all come together. I find it really hard to think beyond the bit we are covering before we move to the next location and do the same. And I am sad about the Irish people that were killed in Tunisia. Well, about all the people killed on that beach by the crazy gunman.'

I give her a hug and pour her tea into her very big mug. 'So, to try to find Ani's story, let's make our own story,' I say. 'We are in the row behind a big table watching a card game at a historical casino that has memories of the big games of the last thousand or so years.'

As she pours my tiny cup of coffee, she adds, 'And we know this is an important game. It's not just a Greek house of cards, but a European house of cards and Greece could potentially take its cards and go home or be kicked out of the casino.'

Non-giggly Sinead is here and I love it when we're creative like this. I continue, 'Yes, big odds for all. A new radical left prime minister who has promised to end Greek austerity but whom Europe wants to nail to the deal of his predecessor. The other side must be thinking that if they give Greece a special card, someone else will want one next.'

Sinead sips her tea and says, 'Maybe it was a promise he shouldn't have made because he couldn't keep it. Politicians everywhere do that don't they? But other European prime ministers have elections too and it's electoral suicide if they overpromise to their voters.'

Sinead makes great Greek coffee. I say, 'Europe is already marketing the referendum as a choice for Greece between staying with the euro or returning to the drachma. It's not that simple. Most Greeks want to belong to the European Union but while we're filming we're seeing unemployment and poverty.'

She sees my empty cup and starts making me another coffee. I continue rambling, 'And now after the expiry of the current bailout, the Prime Minister will put the question to the people for a vote. If he wins, he'll be able to tell Europe that he has a fresh mandate and that Greece doesn't need to stick to what his predecessor promised. That he wants a fresh card deal.'

She adds more sugar to her cup and takes it over to the stove. She's stirring and talking. 'Yes, but Greece has played the same opening card for a long time: "*Our austerity has to be fixed before we can start any deep reforms.*" So, Greece wants to sit at the big table but the others don't trust it to play with real money yet. Greece says, *"Yes, we know we have not been able to meet our debt levels and sure, our monetary policy has been really slack (we give credit to anyone) and yes, we know there was massive tax evasion and yes, we agree, the government spent too much, and yes, even we can't believe our own economic data."* I'm chuckling, not because of what she said, but because of her accent. I don't have to say anything; she starts laughing too. 'The only place that takes me seriously here is our pub,' she says as she refills my cup.

'Thank you. Coming up, it looks as though we'll have an equally interesting time. Referendum around the corner and bills worth around eight billion to be repaid. What do you think of the argument that Germany was never forced to pay enough to Greece for the damage it caused in Greece in World War Two?'

'I think two things. First, Germany should have paid more to Greece. Second, there's no winner in a war tragedy. The world order changed so quickly after the war. The West wanted Germany on board to fight communism, so it said, "*Let's stuff our long-time allies, the Greeks.*"'

I get some sausages, bacon, eggs, mushrooms and tomatoes. She starts chopping. I also find some yoghurt, banana, peaches and nectarines.

She looks up. 'Do we have to eat healthy first?'

I answer, 'Trust me and try to think of it as delicious and local.'

She keeps chopping. 'That is the thing, isn't it? Trust.'

I cut some brown bits out of a banana. 'How so?'

'The wars that countries won or lost centuries ago are not forgotten during a current card game.' I pour some yoghurt into our bowls. 'There are still people sitting at the table who remember, or are paid to remember, all the previous card games and what they want to win back. Not much trust around the table.' I drizzle the honey. She continues, 'And many countries not at the table have players playing for them.'

I throw on the chopped fruit. We start eating. I ask, 'So how are our Ani-stories part of a big carpet rather than a side rug?'

'You are looking for Teo. I am looking for my daideó. My ma wept when she talked about him and your yiayia sobbed when she asked you to find Teo. She has a bad case of the blues and Daideó's time in Greece changed him and brought shame upon the family. Both our family events happened at around the same time.'

'So there are story threads in that carpet,' I say. 'The biggest things for each of us are our grandparents' stories. And I'll throw in an apology; what I initially thought was a tenuous Irish-Greek link for you seems to be a good one for both of us to explore together. Another thread is Odysseus and another thread is that both Ireland and Greece had bitter civil wars that still linger.'

She is whirlpooling all the food in her bowl with her spoon. She holds up an immense dollop of everything as she starts cooking the mushrooms and tomatoes in a different pan. I am nearly ready to lift out the almost perfect eggs. We plate the food together. 'Wait, I'll Instagram this,' I say.

She starts eating. 'And here, when people who lived through the Civil War tell me about it, I see they are still in pain. Before I talked to these people, I thought: *the Greeks and their grudges.* That was diminishing branding of mine, wasn't it?'

'Yep,' I say. This is a grim conversation to have over such delicious food. 'I see pain in the photographs. Desperate faces in a line behind barbed wire fences. Strangulated corpses hanging from trees. Mass graves. Men, women and children, huddled and hungry.'

'Perfect eggs and Ma loves the Insta. We are both going to be really pushed in the next month. Shall we trust each other?'

'Worth a try. Before I go chasing down too many rabbit warrens, I want to find out as much as I can from home about pre-Australian Yiayia. She was so young and I was really moved by the photographs of the children.'

'And I want to do the same with pre-and post-Greece Daideó. His father fought for an independent Ireland, so why did he fight alongside the British?'

'And why did the British, still at war with Germany, arm Nazi collaborators to help them against demonstrators who were supporting the British-assisted resistance movement? They killed young Greek children.'

She smiles and says, 'Back to the casino and our story rugs that we want to weave into the Greek story carpet. A work-in-progress. Two gorgeous female rugs (a young one and a slightly older one) roll into a casino together. They both have only ever used natural dyes. "*Got any jobs for rugs?*" they ask the manager. "*Only one vacancy at the moment for under that table near the carpet,*" says the manager. A rug asks, "*Does it matter what age or gender the applicant is?*" The manager replies, "*We don't discriminate on age or gender here.*" The rugs confer. "*We'll take it,*" they say. "*But I've only got one vacancy,*" repeats the manager. "*Give us a one-month trial and if any customers notice two rugs rather than one you can sack us.*" The manager agrees. A month goes by and no customers report any problems. Some centuries later, when a manager looks under the table, there is only one beautiful big old carpet with some really interesting knots and threads in it.'

Jo

Sunday sleep in? Dream on.

'Jo Jo, would you like a cup of coffee in the garden?' Da's voice floats up from the back door. He must be back from church. No. Go away. I am enjoying a little bit more than just a two-dollar pizza with Vasilios. Then we are planning a post-prandial cigarette and whatever pleasure follows that. 'Jo Jo, it's such a beautiful morning. We have some warm pastries and Padraig and I have bought that expensive coffee that you like so much.' I do not care if you have bought a sexy home-based barista to go with it, I am very dreamy, very busy and very happy. He is knocking on the door now. I can smell the coffee. He must be wafting it up the stairs. 'We're sitting by the shed,' Da adds, in case I cannot find them.

Something is now wrong with Vasilios; he suddenly has Padraig's ears. Time to face the day. However, first, given the abrupt circumstances of my waking, a by-myself cigarette in my small side garden is called for. Mine, mine, mine.

I am still in a dream state as I make my way from my world to theirs. There they are sitting in the garden together around a fully-set breakfast table, cloth included. A silver coffee plunger sits centre stage. Not as interesting as my scene with Vasilios, but fascinating in its own way. I look around for Kevin McCloud.

'Good morning and God bless you,' says Padraig, beaming.

I do not think he would bless the closing moments of my dream. 'How is the Grand Design Project coming along?' I ask.

Da is pouring coffee into little cups with saucers. 'Well, that is a thing,' replies Padraig. 'We are a bit stuck.'

'Surely not. Two of the finest minds in the neighbourhood.'

'Yes, there is that,' Padraig says, as he ponders the thought. 'However, brilliance can be crippling.'

'Jo Jo, we simply have too many ideas,' says Da, as he hands me my coffee. 'Padraig was praying about it at church this morning.'

As I settle myself near the pastries, I respond, 'Then surely God will provide.'

Padraig is quick on the uptake. 'God suggested that we should look right under our noses and utilise the wisdom, knowledge, experience and expertise that we have right here.'

Da takes over. 'Jo Jo, will you help us?'

I did not expect this. A part of me wants to say, '*Yes, yes*' but another part, who has worked with some really loopy clients, is on full alert. 'Da, help you in what way?' I ask, as I begin eating a very tasty almond and walnut pastry.

'Perhaps look at our drawings.'

In my mind, I'm thinking of the core precepts of my already named, but as yet unwritten textbook, 'Essential Skills for Designing with Loopy Clients'. According to my text, at this stage, we should not go near scope, budget, schedule or style; however, we could try to take a step towards the design goals. 'What will be the purpose of the revitalised shed?' I ask, as I savour the syrup on my fingers. 'And "revitalised shed" is not quite right, is it?'

'We've been drawing pictures of the building's exterior,' says Padraig. He hands me a pile of sketches of grand garden buildings that could exist in many of the world's major cities as civic monuments.

'You are so far ahead of me,' I say. 'At times of such advanced thinking, it can be useful to pause and reflect on the proposed purpose of the space.'

They are each tucking into their food. 'It is for Peia to be happy in,' responds Da. Padraig nods his agreement. 'To help bring her back,' Da adds.

'Then maybe the building should be a kind of greenhouse to nurture Mama.' Concurring nods from both of them. 'So, we need to think about what might make her feel nurtured and happy.' It was a question to which I wish I had the answer both now and in the past. I continue, 'How about we make a list of those things. At this stage, we will write down every idea. No questions asked.'

Padraig produces a notebook and pen, hands them to me and commences. 'Angel. It was his shed and without him Peia would never have come here.'

Top of the list. They are each chewing, so I fill the silence. 'What about a Vasilios canvas?' I see them exchange sharp, urgent glances. I smile. 'Just joking. I will not record that one on the list.'

Padraig continues, 'And sunshine, a dance floor and rembetika streaming.' Second, third and fourth.

'And Beth,' says Da. I add her to our list. 'Books. Classics, mostly Greek and Irish. And some reminders of Anna. And you. Your art,' Da adds. Interesting, and added.

'I could do some big, bold screen prints of her girl pirates,' I suggest.

'We need a wide window and lots of glass, so that she can see the birds, our orange tree and the cypress tree,' Da says.

I start nibbling on my second pastry. We can call this meal brunch, I decide. Padraig coughs. 'And I think we need some Frankie.' Very interesting, and added.

Da pauses and then says, 'And Josephine.' Very, very interesting. Added.

'And how might we include Mórai Josephine for Mama?' The question seems to be a brunch stopper. I have just broken the rules I established. Da is silent.

Padraig looks at him and says, 'Harry, in keeping with God's guidance this morning, I think it would be a very good time for you to utilise your wisdom, knowledge, experience and expertise. I will go and make some more coffee.' Plunger in hand, he heads into the house.

Da shuffles and commences tentatively, 'I might need to think out loud on this one.' As loud as you like. Scream if it helps. 'You were named Josephine Anna after my mother.' That is not news. 'Anna was named after her too.'

I was there and remember the reasons for that and say, 'Because she was an awesome woman.'

'She was indeed. A great wife to my da and a wonderful mother to Frankie and me. The other day, when I saw your canvases again, I got to thinking about Frankie.' Keep going Da. 'If she had lived, she would have become one of Australia's best fashion designers. Of that, I am sure. She would have been so proud of you and your art.'

I think about my start-stop canvases. Da continues, 'You might not know that Frankie was named after Mórai Josephine's young sister.' I do not know because I have never been told. 'She was also a wonderful sketcher.' I refuse to fill the silence. 'She and Josephine were very active and respected in the fight for a free Ireland. Ma met my da in the same pursuit. The fight was both a fight with the British for independence and a fight not to sign allegiance to the British monarchy. There was also a fight among the fighters about what form the freedom should take.' Da is talking very slowly and sadly and staring at his hands.

'There was a particularly dangerous action proposed that Ma

and Da did not agree with. Many did not agree with it, but her Frankie supported it.' He looks up. There are tears in his eyes. 'Her sister was killed coldly by one, or more than one, of the freedom fighters who did not support the action. By their own people in the fight for a free Ireland.'

As I imagine a younger, bullet-ridden, dead version of Móraí Josephine, I begin to cry. Like Easter Sunday at the hospital, Da stretches out his arms and I go into them. A heaving mess: great big me and little old him.

Da continues, 'She never got over it. She lost her trust in her own people. She and Da came to Australia soon after. She relived it all again when her daughter, your mother, Frankie died. And Peia was with her so much during that time, during your early years.'

Fresh coffee is being poured into my cup by Padraig, who has made his quietest entrance ever. Padraig picks up the story where Da left off. 'When Peia arrived in this garden, through Angel's shed, we did not know anything about her, other than that Angel had been working very hard with some Greeks and others to get her here.'

We might have to call this meal 'brinner'. Padraig offers me a warm pastry and continues. 'All we knew was that she was Angel's grand-niece and a refugee from the Greek Civil War. We knew nothing about that war then. Angel would not reveal any of her personal details. He said that she would tell people what she wanted to tell people, when she was good and ready. She has done so, bit by bit, over the decades.'

Da smiles. 'Ma knew just how to nurture her and they spent much of their time out here with books, birds and plants. To try to impress her, I planted the orange tree. That barely raised an eyebrow. She said that they had a whole field of them at home. I did a little bit better with the cypress tree. They only had one of those.' He sits back in his chair looking relieved. 'Padraig, in keeping with God's guidance this morning, I think it would be a very good time for you to utilise your wisdom, knowledge, experience and expertise in relation to Vasilios.'

Padraig looks as though God has spoken. 'I liked the boy', he states.

'You never met him,' I say.

'I was the chaplain to the art school.'

'The art school had a chaplain?'

'In the seventies, the art school could have done with a cathedral full of chaplains. Not many of its students came to me, so I used to go to them. At one exhibition, I was particularly taken with some of the abstract work. My core business is the abstract.' I had never thought of it like that; of Padraig's career being in the abstract. 'At this one show, I bought a piece for my room. Twenty dollars from my stipend. At the time, of course, I didn't know that he was a person of interest to both you and Peia. I talked to the young man at the exhibition. He was struggling with many of the same concepts I had struggled with on my journey towards pacifism.'

It is hard to imagine Padraig struggling with concepts, he always seems so certain. 'I was surprised when I heard Peia's reaction to your pizza outing. Of course, that sort of reaction was often Peia's first reaction to things. But I slowly realised that the cause of her concern was the maker of my art. I liked the canvas on my wall. Peia never saw my room and I thought that it would all blow over, as so many things did with Peia. When it didn't, one day I quizzed her about what it was she knew about Vasilios that made him so unsuitable. She told me in no uncertain terms that his parents were traitors in the Civil War. Despite my best efforts, no further details were ever forthcoming. Angel was right, Peia tells people what she wants to tell people when she is good and ready.'

'Da, do you know any more?' I ask. 'No.'

'Padraig, it is your canvas then.' 'It is yours now.'

Da stands up, 'I should go in and talk with Peia.' I resist my project coordinator's urge to do a wrap up of the meeting and ask if we have left anything out. Teo is not on the list.

Peia

'*Kalispera*, Theía,' says Theo. Theo. Teo. I nod and smile as best as I can. Some of Calandra's wind is still with me. I point and Theo sees the galaktoboureko. 'Yes, please,' he replies. 'A slice for you too?' It is on the 'Maysa No List', which Calandra says is nonsense. I have had more than allowed today (none is allowed). I shake my head. He pulls up a stool next to me and starts eating. 'Ah, wonderful. Who made this?' I wish I knew and I wish I could tell him. '*Sygnómi*, sorry, I shouldn't ask you "who" questions.'

He seems very happy. 'I went to a party last night. I sang in a scratch-together band. Not as good as the musicians at your party but not too bad. And they let me play a borrowed guitar. It was my friend's girlfriend's guitar. This galaktoboureko is as good as my mother's. She must never learn that I said that.'

He sits, eating quietly. 'You know how I was telling you about my good mate who died.' I nod. 'I got to thinking about him last night at the party. I haven't let him go. I wasn't in a good space at the time of his burial. So angry. And I don't feel good about that now. It was all so fast and too soon for me perhaps?'

'Yes,' I say.

He smiles. 'Thought so. And it was really cool the way you just said "yes" without a great song and dance about it. And I don't have a clipboard to give you a tick. A hug?'

'Yes.' That's me again. And he is hugging me. A long hug. Such a good hugger.

He sits down again. 'I skyped Anna this morning and told her about the party. She told me about Adriana. One of your crazy pirates.' I like Theo's medicine and he's the only one who gets away with this sort of bedside manner. 'And I sang to her. A song about rain at midnight.' Rain and midnight? I question internally. 'Would you like me to sing to you?'

If it's good enough for Anna, it's good enough for me. 'Yes. Please.'

'Okay. I'll sing the "Yes, Please" song.' He starts singing, "Yes, Please" to the tune of "Twinkle, Twinkle, Little Star".

Yes please yes please yes please yes,
Yes please yes please yes please yes.

He has a lovely deep voice. It would be so good for rembetika.

'Like to join in?' He asks me. I would love to join in but the wind has gone very calm. 'Just maybe hum along then?' I am stuck. Like a cow in a bog. 'Theía,' he's louder, 'Odysseus, Grace and Adriana would all have had days when they couldn't do astounding things. Days when humming was the thing to do.' He starts singing again.

Yes please yes please yes please yes.

Then I hear sound coming out of me, me humming to his singing. I am humming with him.

Yes please yes please yes please yes.

'Don't stop,' he booms. 'We are going to sing and hum the roof off this hive.' And here I am. Queen bee in a forest. Humming. Loudly. I don't want to stop. Except for the dancing with Calandra, this is the best I have felt since the night that Teo came back. Harry is standing at the door. I stop.

He says, 'Don't stop. Please don't stop! Hello, Theo. I love the song!'

'Hello, to you too. The song is a new composition of mine and dedicated to Theía Peia.'

'Can I sit and hear a little more of it?' Harry asks.

I'm not sure I can do it again.

'Well, it is actually composed for a trio,' says Theo. 'If Theía is happy with you joining our group, I am. Are you a hummer or a singer?'

'I would like to learn to hum as well as Peia, so can I do that?' he asks. I nod.

'Okay. We'll start on three. Together now, one, two, three.'

Yes please yes please yes please yes.

'Louder hummers, I can't hear you.'

Yes please yes please yes please yes.

And there is Harry, the music to my dance, humming away. We hum and Theo sings until the twinkles come right out of that little star.

'Harry and Theía, would you like to try the words?' Harry looks at me and asks, 'Peia?'

The stuck cow feeling is sticking, but an unstuck buzzing bee feeling is also saying, *if you are going to unstick anything Peia, Harry is your man.*

'Harry, you start singing with me. Theía you start humming and if you can join in with the words, go for it. Together now. One, two, three.'

Yes please yes please yes please yes.

'Great humming. Theía.'

Yes please yes please yes please yes.

'Great singing, Harry.'

Yes please yes please yes please yes.

'Great singing, Harry and Theía.'

Yes please yes please yes please yes.

'Great singing Harry, Theía and Theo.'

The trio is singing the words. My letters and words are joined. I'm part of a band. Singing these two little words over and over again is making me feel so happy. We sing on and on and on, until Jo Jo is singing and clapping next to me.

A great wave has carried me to a crest.

Theo stops and says, 'Great singing Harry, Theía, Theo and Jo. "The Yes Please Quartet." A new combination.'

'We should launch Theo's new song and quartet. Drinks?' suggests Harry, as he heads towards the kitchen.

Jo Jo is calm. More so than I've seen her since Teo came back. If I was still smoking, now would be the time for us to slip out to her courtyard. Unfortunately, that pleasure like galaktoboureko is not on Maysa's approved list.

Harry returns with some glasses and drinks. 'Promise we won't tell Maysa tomorrow,' he says, as he puts a little ouzo by my left side.

'Da, would you like me to pop in tomorrow when Maysa comes?' asks Jo Jo.

'Peia?' he replies.

'*Yes please yes please yes please yes,*' I sing. They laugh with me.

'And Calandra popped into the garden when I was there with Padraig and she would like to come tomorrow too?' As long as she is nice to Maysa. Different approaches. I nod. 'And when Padraig heard that Calandra wanted to come, he said that, as part of your team, he would like to come too. He promised not to talk about anything you might disagree with.' Then he will be totally silent.

Keep Ithaca always in your mind.

I nod. My mind is in the now. Harry rises, glass in hand. 'Quartet, a hundred thousand welcomes. Theo, a hundred thousand thanks. Peia, a hundred thousand blessings. To us and our new song.'

A blend of 'Cheers', 'Yamas' and 'Sláinte' rings out. As Jo Jo moves to help me with my little glass, I let her, though my fingers seem as if they are mine again.

'We could try something else,' announces Theo. Will he ever stop? 'How about "Happy Sunday to Us" to the tune of "Happy Birthday"? Here's how it goes.'

Happy Sunday to us, Happy Sunday to us,

Happy Sunday, Happy Sunday, Happy Sunday to us.

'Humming or singing, it doesn't matter. One, two, three.'

I am humming a bit and singing a bit. This song takes a bit more joining. If Anna could see us now, just like in ancient times, humming and singing. After we do it a few times, there is no longer any leader. We are with each other and I never want it to end. We slow down. We are happy to be slow. Quite deliberately slow and quite deliberately happy. *My homeland is in sight.*

Anna

It's late and we're in the office looking at Jimmi's footage of the clashes in Syntagma Square, outside parliament house, during the debate on the latest proposed austerity measures. It's crackly black and white imagery and feels older than it is. It looks like what I've seen of December 1944, except then the protestors numbered around 60,000 and now they number around 12,000. And there were British tanks then.

Jimmi has a great eye for the visual. The ancient democratic symbols are clear in the background. In the foreground, the protestors are hurling Molotov cocktails and rocks. In the middle ground, the traffic lights are flashing but they may as well be turned off. From the wings, the riot-clad police move to disperse the summer-dressed protestors, using pepper spray and tear gas. Jimmi is close to the police. Very brave. An outer-Sami day.

'Well done, Jimmi,' I say. 'The police can disperse the moment but not the story.'

He replies, 'I've shown this to Ani. She seemed happy with it. Well, happier than her happiness with my work to date. She might even let me take off my L-plates.'

'We'd better mark the occasion then,' Sinead announces, pulling some beers from the fridge and passing them out. We clink our bottles.

'But wait, there's more,' says Jimmi. 'Would you like to see what might be the start of my Ani-project?' Sinead and I nod and pull up some comfy chairs. 'I'll use the big screen,' Jimmi says. 'The soundtrack is a band from my hometown.'

Lights outs. Beers in. Screen and sound on. Heavy metal music thumps, as the scene opens on a clip of the recent riots.

Soldiers, civilians, Hellas at war.

Sinead yells, 'I saw this band in Belfast last year!' The music is familiar but I can't quite nail it.

Descendants of Sparta, Athens and Crete, Look north, ready to fight.

Footage rolls of the newly erected razor-wire fence along the Hungary-Serbian border before cutting to people partying on the Greek islands and then to refugees in boats off the Greek islands. Jimmi has incorporated his May Day footage of the locals coming and going about their normal business while the blue wheelie bins, set alight by the precision aim of the cocktail throwers, burn. Next, a more recent clip of the police appears. The camera is even closer to the action this time.

Enemies charge from the hills, To arms! Facing defeat!

I suddenly remember the band from a date with a heavy-metal music enthusiast. He thought I'd love 'the Greek stuff'. I didn't get him or the 'Greek stuff' in that context, but I love what Jimmi's done here.

Now, images of Greek pensioners queuing outside a bank and people queueing for the launch of the Apple watch.

Time after time,

Force their enemies back to the line.

The reopening of the Greek banks appears in one frame, the executives responsible for the Volkswagen emission violations in another.

Strike hard, the tables have turned, Drive them back over the hills.

Now animated images appear, presented as card games. The

first card: the resignation of the Finance Minister. The second card: an image of the new Finance Minister.

Just like their ancestors ages ago, Fought in the face of defeat.

Sinead says, 'Jimmi, that's our card game at the casino that you don't know about.' The film continues to roll. More animations. The majority parliamentary vote for the bailout plan. The pack being reshuffled for a cabinet reshuffle.

Blood of King Leonidas.

Indicating his beer is empty, Jimmi pauses the film and says, 'Ani wants her documentaries to somehow change the way audiences think. Change their minds and preconceptions, right?'

I nod. 'When I studied journalism, documentaries were defined as the creative interpretation of reality.'

Sinead heads to the fridge as she adds, 'And Ani focuses on Greek stories that are universal.'

Jimmi continues, 'I've only been in Greece a short time. I was shocked initially when I saw the effects of the Greek Financial Crisis on the streets but then I got used to it. When I saw the refugees on the islands, I vowed I would never get used to it. Now the whole world is used to it. It's just more news.'

'Hence, the animation?' I ask.

'Yes, I want to lure people in with my beautiful and brilliant animations before I hit them on the head and transform their lives.'

'Go you!' says Sinead handing out some more beers.

'I want people to be moved by this creative interpretation of the current Greek reality. Interval is over,' Jimmi announces, unpausing the footage. The sacking of the No Vote parliamentarians is illustrated as cards being removed from the deck and tossed on the ground.

'Jimmi, you need our beautiful big old carpet on the ground,' I say.

He replies, 'I don't know about that either.' Next, we see

animations of Greek soldiers holding endless money bags, jumping out of the front of a Trojan horse. At the same time, faceless characters feed a sausage line of money bags into the horse's rear. It's brilliant. I'm laughing even as I feel that I should not laugh. Clever Jimmi. He has mixed comedy and tragedy. I've dropped my defences. He's luring me in before changing my life.

Call to arms banners fly in the wind, For the glory of Hellas.

Images follow of the Trojan malware virus of January this year. One of them has a Trojan horse head with a viper's tail. 'Jimmi, your drawings are awesome!' Sinead comments, echoing my thoughts. Jimmi flips to news that Instagram has overtaken Twitter. It shows people cruising on yachts around Greece. Then to Twitter commenting on the refugee crisis. Next, film footage and the Twitter commentary on the boat that capsized while carrying eight hundred and fifty refugees on its crossing between Turkey and Greece.

There's no surrender! There's no retreat!

Then we move to volcanic ash over Bali and consumer outrage as flights are delayed.

Endure six days of rain.

Images of '*Je suis Charlie*', follows.

Call to arms, banners fly in the wind.

'Wow,' Sinead and I chorus.

She adds, 'Jimmi, you have woven some really interesting knots and threads into the casino's beautiful big old carpet.'

'It's early days, but a few dots might be joining,' he says.

There's no surrender, there's no retreat.

Peia

At the request of the women, the priest has called a meeting in the church to discuss the information we were presented with at the town meeting. This time, the commander will not be in attendance. After dinner, we trek up our path towards the silent siren. Officially, we are going to a special evening service. Some sheep are grazing by the church, which could do with a whitewash. Such things have not been given high priority of late.

The priest welcomes Mama and Theía Trenna. After a quiet chat, Mama suggests that Agnete and I look after the children outside. I know where I'd prefer to be. An excited Teo and Adelphos run off after the other children who are already chasing the sheep. Agnete and I head towards where some sheep have already been cornered by the children. A breakaway group of children is sitting astride the fence and looking longingly at the forest. 'Let's tell them a story,' I suggest quickly and call out, 'Who would like to be the Cyclops, the giant?' Adelphos and another boy appear immediately by my side. They can both be the Cyclops. Agnete tells them to work out who will be the bottom and who will be the top and to find a big eye for the centre of their forehead. They accept their orders like professional soldiers.

I want to be inside the church listening to the discussion. 'Who would like to be Odysseus?' I call out. Teo's hand alone shoots straight up. I thought there would be more volunteers.

'What about Odysseus's crew?' Lots of hands are raised. We have our cast. Agnete starts separating the actors; Polyphemus, the Cyclops, is placed in one corner and Odysseus and his crew in another. The sheep, not wanting to be cornered, head to the middle. I can sense the church breathing.

I start the story. 'Odysseus and his crew were sailing home from Troy.' Agnete has the team rowing. Not all in time. But rowing. 'They see an island and decide to stop and find some food.' Teo and his crew are miming my instructions. 'They climb up a hill, find a cave full of food and drink, take their fill and fall asleep.' The actors are fully engaged. 'Polyphemus, the Cyclops, returns to the cave with his giant sheep.' Adelphos (the bottom of the giant) staggers in behind some normal-sized sheep. 'Polyphemus rolls a huge stone into place to shut the entrance of the cave.' Agnete shapes two actors into a ball as the stone.

A little ahead of my commentary, Adelphos starts staggering around in a rage. The top boy hangs on for dear life. Adelphos grabs two members of Odysseus's crew and he and his top pretend to eat them. Agnete ushers the eaten crew members to the side.

I continue, 'Odysseus needs to think of a plan.' Teo puts on an excellent thinking face, placing his finger on his chin. I resume the story, 'The next morning, Polyphemus eats two more crew members for breakfast.' Agnete moves two more of the cast to the side. Teo is sitting by himself with the thinking face anyone would have if two more members of their crew had just been eaten. 'Polyphemus rolls away the stone and takes his sheep to graze.' The stone rolls itself away and the sheep are running ahead of a wobbling Adelphos.

I carry on, 'In the cave, Odysseus and his men find a large branch, carve it to a point, and hide it.' Teo's remaining crew members mime these actions. 'At the end of the day, Polyphemus returns home with the sheep, blocks the cave with the stone and eats two more crew members.' This is acted out with the giant's head sporting an even bigger pine cone as an eye. 'Odysseus then offers Polyphemus some wine that he has brought from his ship.' Teo hands the wine to the giant in a cup-shaped hat. 'Polyphemus drinks the wine and relaxes.' Adelphos and his passenger slowly slump down onto the soil. 'Polyphemus thanks Odysseus for the wine and asks him his name. Odysseus replies, "My Name is Nobody." Polyphemus falls asleep and Odysseus and his crew take a sharpened branch and poke it in Polyphemus's eye.' This is acted out and the huge pine cone falls dramatically to the ground.

'A howling, blind Polyphemus awakens his Cyclop neighbours, who demand "Who has done this to you?"' A group of formerly eaten, now recycled, crew members, stand on each other's shoulders and hold pine cones to act this scene out. 'Polyphemus roars "Nobody Did It To Me." The neighbours exit and Polyphemus goes back to sleep. Overnight, Odysseus ties each of his men to the belly of a sheep.' With our normal-sized sheep, this scene is impossible to act out in this production, so when Polyphemus awakes, the cast simply hover out of blind Polyphemus's way, while he feels the normal-sized sheep for human passengers.

'Odysseus and his crew then exit the cave with Polyphemus and rush back to their ship.' Agnete has all the cast rushing and then rowing. It seems that more of the Cyclops's former breakfast food are alive and well again. In the twilight, out of the corner of my eye, I see the women emerging from the church. They stand as one and watch the spectacle. I need to finish the story. 'From the boat, Odysseus can't help himself and calls out to Polyphemus, "It was not Nobody but me Odysseus, who blinded and fooled you".' There is a combined sigh from the church. Bad call Odysseus. From behind me, Mama places her hands on my shoulders and kisses the back of my neck. I think she might be crying. I would like to cry but quickly the other women clap and the priest comes over and blesses all of us (even the sheep) before we head back down the valley.

Jo

Maysa has just reported on Ma's progress to Team Mama. So, Da, Padraig and I are all late for our onsite shed revitalisation meeting. I am grinning like the parent of a winning student on Speech Day. The Team-Mama summit was longer than expected mostly because of good news from the speech, occupational and physiotherapists. Mama sat beaming in the centre of us like a child at school who had won their first-ever prize. At last, lots of ticked boxes and a good report card.

Maysa was the most optimistic she has been since the night Anna left. She guided us through terms such as, 'flaccidity', 'spasticity', 'complex movements' (there have been some) and 'normal function'. However, she reminded us several times that while Mama (and her team) have made a great start at home rehabilitation, it is unlikely that she will return to fully normal function. Maysa emphasised that the work is, and will continue to be, exhausting for the patient, progress will take time and there will be ordinary days, backward days and forward days.

I admire my sketches in which I had tried to capture the ideas from my last garden discussion with Da and Padraig: a place to tempt Mama back; a happiness site; a nurturing greenhouse; a sunshine trap; a space to gaze at birds and trees; a book nook for Greek and Irish classics; and a cultural place for dance and music and some of my art. The space should also have reminders of Angel, Beth, Josephine, Frankie and Anna, as well as Da, Padraig and Mama's friends. I had lost myself while I was doing the sketches. This crazy shed might just be a good idea.

Padraig appears with Theo by his side who asks, 'Can you swap my Theía Peia roster for tomorrow? I've just had a text from work, it's no longer my rostered day off.'

'Sure,' I respond. I have some work to do tomorrow, but nothing urgent.

'Great,' he replies. 'I know this is a very select project management group, but as a builder, I might be able to help.' He looks at us both. 'In fact, I know I can help.'

I love his confidence. I wish I'd had the same amount at his age. 'Great,' I reply, as Padraig claps his hands together. 'I am sure Da will be glad for the help.'

'I'll go and check with him first,' Theo says and heads back inside.

Padraig pulls up a garden chair and starts looking at my sketches. '*Hatchet! Hatchet!*' he cries. '*Hatchet? Hatchet?*' I ask.

'Brilliant. Brilliant,' he explains. 'The whole shebang.'

'Thanks, Padraig, but it's not the whole shebang yet. I am a bit stuck on how to bring some of the people into it through Mama's eyes, rather than mine. For example, I know how to bring Mórai Josephine in as my grandmother but not as Mama's friend. Does that make sense?'

'Yes, yes,' he replies. He takes a deep breath. 'The way in which her sister died was enough for her to question her God, her people and life itself.'

'Her God?'

'Yes, when I first met her she was not attending church. A born-again Atheist.' He laughs.

'I was door-knocking in the parish. Actually, I was knocking on the doors of the non-attenders of the parish. She opened one of those doors, invited me in for scones and told me I would be welcome as long as I didn't mention religion or Ireland. That was the start of my first ever proper friendship.'

'How was it a proper friendship?', I ask.

'No bullshit,' Padraig answers. I had no idea Padraig could utter that word. 'We were there for each other and we laughed and cried together. Her sister's death was brutal and carried out by someone fighting for a free Ireland. Someone Frankie and Josephine had trusted. She found her sister betrayed, tarred, feathered and dead.'

'But she made my Irish dancing costumes and First Communion dress,' I say.

'She did not want you to grow up with any Civil War bitterness. By then, she thought she had passed too much sadness on to her own children and she was determined not to do so with you. Particularly given what Peia had brought with her from Greece through that shed. She wanted to protect you,' Padraig replies.

'And what exactly did Mama bring with her through that shed?'

'Another Civil War. Peia never talked about it to me, but she and Josephine talked and cried with each other. They had a safe zone. Josephine emerged from her Civil War. Peia's has resurfaced with her stroke.'

'How did Móraí Josephine emerge?'

'She was an amazingly resilient woman. I think we had a safe zone and trusted each other too. We had both seen terrifying things. We talked about our nightmares, our depression. We could spot when each other was withdrawing. We knew when either of us had seen or heard something that had sent us back. It was a club of two when Harry and Frankie were children.'

'And Mama was like that too?'

'Is like that. And people who haven't had the same experience just have to be there for her.'

'Is it post-traumatic stress?' I wonder aloud.

'These days it has that name,' he answers. 'Josephine's

memories intensified when her other Frankie, your mother, died. Peia was there for her. These days we would say she was there twenty-four seven for her. Maybe she was not there enough for you. But Harry was there for each of you. It is a wonder he is so normal.' He laughs at his comment. Da and Theo join us.

Theo is measuring the shed. Da and I are hugging. He says, 'I think she is going to be all right. I think we are going to be all right.'

'*Hatchet. Hatchet*,' I answer. 'Now Anna just needs to find Teo.'

'To be sure. To be sure,' affirms Padraig.

Peia

I am with Mama, Teo, Theía Trenna and Adelphos. We are walking in single file, joined together in slowness and soundlessness. I feel a mix of adventure and responsibility.

Just before we left home, I climbed up to the top storey of our house. To be alone for a moment, to savour the place that had once overflowed with the village at Teo's party. I wanted to freeze time, to capture the sounds of others in our house and the sight of our orange trees and cypress tree. Mama crept up behind me, put her arms around me and whispered, 'You can do this. Papa and I know that you can do this.'

Greek planes have been dropping bombs nearby for the last few days. This is the closest the war has been to me so far. Some of the families who attended the recent village meeting have been killed in their own homes by bombs dropped by their own government. The decision about what to do with the children is not a decision any more. It is a resolution. Our village is going to be destroyed. Our homes.

I have been concentrating on showing Mama that I can do this. That I can be a free flying stork and not a Quitter Bird. That I can care for my precious brother and his friend while Mama and Theía Trenna join the effort to finish the war. That I can hold both these little boys and not let them go until the Greek planes stop bombing grandmothers, mothers and children.

In the twilight, I smell the new spring flowers edging the path and make out some flowers on the other paths that weave through our steep valley. So many paths. I can only just see the outlines of other groups of women and children heading up to the church before us. Normally, at this time, smells of cooking would be wafting to us. Tonight, there is no scent of lamb, dill or lemon. In hope, we all stop, raise our noses up and sniff, but no smells of cooking permeate the air. The path forks and we turn towards the church. Some people have already gathered.

As Adelphos sees the church, he falls out of formation, runs ahead and leaps into the air. His howls shatter the silence and scatter the sheep. Some fence wire has caught his left hand on our side of the fence while his body is on the other side of the fence. He is still in one piece but blood is oozing from his hand. We move quickly. His mother places her handkerchief over the gash. I am now kneeling on the ground next to Adelphos with one hand over his mouth. So much for a covert exit. In this natural amphitheatre, his cries could alert all of Greece that a group of small children and a few teenagers are about to commence a dangerous walk in the dark to a new country.

Everyone is gathering around. Adelphos's wails have set off many of the younger children whose mothers have only recently convinced them of the advantages of heading off without them on a big, exciting adventure towards safety. Teo is patting Adelphos like a puppy, repeating, 'Adelphos, look at me!' Teo makes a silly face.

'Adelphos, can you make a face like that?' I ask. Adelphos's cries subside briefly as he scrunches up his face. It looks more painful than silly. Mama and Theía Trenna examine our patient's hand. Their latest makeshift bandage does not turn red immediately. Mama briefly lifts up the bandage. The gash is large but the blood flow is easing.

Next to us, Vaska produces a small bottle from his pack. 'This might hurt a bit, but it should help it heal,' he tells Adelphos.

Sniffing the mixture, Theía Trenna pours a little onto a cloth and says to us, 'Keep him distracted.'

Teo whispers to Adelphos, 'I am going to beat you to the edge of the world.' 'I am faster so that will never happen,' Adelphos replies.

As Theía Trenna dabs the mixture on the wound, Adelphos screams. Teo whispers loudly to Adelphos, 'If you keep screaming like that I will easily beat you to the edge of the world and to beyond the edge of the next world.'

Adelphos quietens down. 'I will beat you. I will fly if I have to.' Theía Trenna cradles his head as he begins to sob.

Jo

It is early morning in my winter courtyard and I am exhausted. I feel the weight of my dreams. Too much time with a young Vasilios or not enough? At one point in my dream, Vasilios and his mother were sitting in our circle singing, 'Happy Sunday to You'. It all started very well. Mama was the best version of her former self. Theo was leading us while simultaneously measuring each of us with his tape measure. However, when we moved to the 'Yes, Please' song, Mama changed the words to 'No, Thanks' and insisted that Vasilios and his mother sing the words or leave the room. When they refused to do so, she ostracised them, keening like a banshee and dancing around them, until she orbited them out of the front door singing, 'Never, never on a Sunday, a Sunday, a Sunday, cause that's my day of rest.' I watched it all listlessly but, other than refusing to join in her dance, I did nothing to stop her. Does refusing to join in a dance count as an act of resistance?

Today was going to be my 'relinquishing-my-one-cigarette-a-day' day, but as I am already spent, I need the nicotine to ease me into my 'music-and dance-with-Mama' morning. I need to move along. I start when I see her sitting in her approved chair looking out on a wintery street. I spot a banshee. This is not a good way to start the day.

Calandra is my co-worker today. For me, she stands out among Mama's friends, partly because she moves independently.

She has coffee and cake waiting. As she hands me a generous slice of yoghurt cake, she makes a point of telling me, decades after the event, that she was not part of the seventies Vasilios lynch mob. Then straight away, she adds a dollop of cream to my cake. The moment is over in a second. Did she have the same dream last night? Without further explanation, she asks, 'Peia, what music would you like? Something we all know the words to and can dance to?'

We are trying to help Mama find her buried words by singing songs she knows. We are also hoping to bring her mental and physical networks together by dancing. Mama points to her phone, which I fetch. She scrolls through her music and then clicks on her rembetika collection. I ask, 'Mama, you want to move to that?'

'Yes, please,' she replies. Stupid question.

Calandra pauses and then says, 'We can dance to anything, of course.' Mama clicks on a song. It is of course in Greek. A funereal song. Why does she do it? Adolescent Jo answers adult Jo, 'To spite you.'

Padraig says that Mama brought a Civil War through Theío Angel's shed and now people just have to be there for her. I am already twitching at the melancholy music. Can I be there for her this morning? She has closed her eyes. Calandra pauses, listens and says, 'Ah, "Night Descending Without Moon".' She begins translating for me.

Peia

Calandra speaks the lyrics, '*The darkness is deep and yet a young man cannot fall asleep.*'

I am a young girl. In our valley. My family is in the circle. My mama. My brother, Teo. His friend, Adelphos. His mother, Theía Trenna. Some people from other families. My papa. He could be that young man who cannot fall asleep. He will fall asleep. There the circles of dancers included everyone. Friends. Enemies.

Calandra continues, *'What could he be waiting for, from dusk until dawn?'*

I am tense. A young man is waiting for the dawn. The time at which executions take place. He is not sure if today is his day. We had such a happy day together when the war against the Germans ended. This is not that day. This young man fought in another war straight after that war.

Calandra is singing, '*The narrow window, is lit by a candle.*'

A candle can be romantic. I would like it if Papa was waiting to see Mama. But this candle does not have a happy ending. A door opens. A door closes. It's the same door. A guard comes in and pushes the young man out. This is where I get stuck. At this prison. However, since the night Anna left, I can't be here now without going there first. My mind insists on taking me into this prison. Through this prison. There is also another prison. For women. I can't see that other prison as clearly.

Jo Jo is next to me. Calandra is singing on my other side. Jo Jo says, 'Calandra, pause. Mama one, two, three, stand.' Now, we are all standing. We shuffle a little. Then we are in a group hug. Jo Jo is humming rembetika. She is even humming it the right way. Soulfully. I am singing in Greek. Lots of right words in a row. I am broken hearted and loud.

Calandra is singing slowly and mournfully in English, '*With a heavy sigh, I wish I could guess, the sorrow in his heart.*'

I can feel and see the sorrow in his heart. His wife. His daughter. His son. The country for which he fought so hard. But I am going to sing and dance through this prison. It is not going to imprison me anymore. I am getting out of this prison. Not the way Papa got out of this prison. But out. Calandra asks, 'Again, Peia?'

I am not a Quitter Bird. 'Yes, please. Again,' I say. Then Calandra is singing in English again, I am singing in Greek and Jo Jo is humming and crying in both languages. She hated Greek at school but she is belting some out now. I look into her wet eyes. I sing, 'Papa. Prison.'

Jo Jo sings, 'Papa. Prison. Where?'

The darkness is deep and yet a young man cannot fall asleep.

Calandra is belting out the lyrics like a blues singer should.

What could he be waiting for, from dusk until dawn?

Jo Jo sings, 'Your brother?' 'My Papa,' I answer.

I wish I could guess, the sorrow in his heart.

I stop. I want to tell Jo Jo the sorrow in my heart. I keep singing in Greek. Calandra translates. 'They hit me and hit me. So hard. So hard. Blood. More blood.'

Jo Jo is all eyes, ears and tears. I have to sing it to her.

'Too much blood to have my own babies.' Move me, winds.

'You were Frankie's. Then mine. I always thought I would lose you too.' Keep translating Calandra. Move me, Grace.

'Find Teo. He ran from the play. Please, please, find him for us.'

Jo

It is hideously early and light. I am onsite, holding my third coffee and second cigarette. I do not care who sees me. Last night, the dreams were even more leaden than before. There was a labyrinthine prison and a minotaur with Vasilios's head and a young boy's body. Calandra, dressed in a kinky guard outfit, winked at me as she gave me a ball of string and pointed me down a staircase. I have been spending too much time searching for Vasilios on social media before bedtime; however, I have not yet found him other than in my dreams.

Here come the boys: Da, Padraig and Theo, who set this ridiculously early hour, as he needs to go to work. He has that early-morning sexy tradie look. Back in the day, I would not have minded if he had whistled at me even if it would have obliged me to flash him the V-sign in return. Padraig is in some sort of builder's costume, complete with hard hat. It is beginning to look like a Village People reunion. Am I still dreaming? This is the first time I have ever seen Padraig out of his priestly garb. Da is in his green dressing gown and four-leaf clover slippers that Anna gave him for a birthday long ago. He is less of a Village Person and more like a child who has turned up at school for the St Patrick's Day Parade in a last-minute costume.

As Theo spreads a paper plan on the ground, he says, largely for the benefit of the other two, 'Jo and I have come up with this. What do you think?' A Jo-Theo collaboration. My design and his floor plan. I would like to think each of us influenced the other.

Da and Padraig do not need to talk to each other. They are like an old married couple who can communicate with gestures and consonants. 'Tch … tch … tch' sounds elicit from Da, as he touches the existing shed.

'Pffh … pffh … pffh,' adds Padraig, pointing to the plan.

'Mmmnnn … mmmnnnn … mmmnnn.' Da paces between the shed and the garden.

'Rrrmmm … rrrmmm … rrrmmm.' Padraig nods at the plan and then the sky. Is he giving thanks for my divine intervention? Theo walks around measuring everything in the garden. 'Elegant!' declares Padraig finally. 'Old but new.'

'Angel, Beth, Josephine and Frankie,' says Da, sighing.

I pull out another cigarette. Padraig produces a lighter from his pocket and lights it for me. Another first. I have my mint tin ashtray. I would like to be smoking with Anna right now. Da pauses, looks me in the eye and speaks, 'Móraí Josephine never found proper peace after she lost her sister in the Irish Civil War. I didn't know how to help her when she was going through that but I know how to help your mama now. Jo Jo, please go to Greece and help Anna find Teo.' Supplicant Da. 'I am best at staying here, looking after Peia and building this for her. You and Anna will make a formidable team over there.'

'And what if we cannot find Teo?' I ask.

Theo says, 'I'm going to Greece for my mother's sixtieth birthday. My father has worn me down. I'll need to be there in the first week of September. I haven't told my parents yet. Or Anna.'

'What about work?' I ask him.

'They will let me take a break. It's a Greek company. They are used to us coming and going.' 'What about this?' I ask, gesturing to our plans.

As he gets ready to leave for work he says, 'My mate's girlfriend is happy to project manage it while I'm away.' I hope that she is still his mate's girlfriend. Is there anything this woman cannot or does not do?

Anna's super-tanned face is suddenly on my phone. She has caught me smoking. I answer. 'Morning Mum!', she calls, as Padraig and Da squeeze into my phone's frame.

She never rings this early. She looks fine but I ask anyway, 'Are you okay?'

'To be sure, to be sure. I'm sorry to ring you so early but you seem to be up and about anyway.'

'Yes, we're having an early meeting of the Shed Revitalisation Committee before Theo goes to work.'

I think I see her preen a little. 'Hello, Theo. Hello, Da. Hello, Padraig.' 'Theo's just left for work. Why are you ringing so late? So early?'

'Look at this, Mum.' She holds up a flyer with bold abstract images with a 'V' woven through them. It is unmistakably Vasilios's work. I have searched every social media site in the world.

'Jesus, Mary and Joseph,' Padraig utters.

'What's for you won't pass you,' Da affirms.

'Da, Padraig, I need some time alone with my daughter.' They scurry off like a chorus thick with sonorous speechless sounds. Squinting at the flyer, I inhale my nicotine hungrily before asking, 'Who, what, when, where, and why?'

Anna rummages in her bag. 'I need a cigarette too. Ani is getting some drinks but that might take forever because she knows everyone in Athens.' She lights up her cigarette. I see the city behind her. She begins, 'Ani and I just came from work. She was looking at my story on the reopening of the Stock Exchange and its plunge in value. In my story, alongside the currency fall, I showed her my chart of the week: refugee and migrant numbers peaking as the Stock Exchange falls. The crisis within the crisis.' Mama would love this lively view of Anna and Athens. 'I have those photographs you sent me of Vasilios's canvases pinned to a board near my desk. Ani saw them for the first time tonight.'

'Indeed I did,' a new voice joins the conversation. It has to be Ani. 'Hello, Anna's mother!' 'Hello, Anna's boss!' I reply.

'Too early for a drink for you I guess?' she says as she and Anna clink glasses.

I answer, 'Yes but I might be able to join you for one or two next month.'

'Mum, you've decided to come?'

'Anna, I think I have and if you finish the story about that flyer, it might help my decision.'

'We can both finish the story,' Ani says. 'I saw the abstract images and asked Anna if it was recent work.'

'I replied that it was ancient work,' Anna says.

'I then added that I love his work and Anna asked if I knew the artist. I answered that I knew someone who did.'

Anna continues, 'She then produced this flyer from a pile of papers on her desk.'

'My mother had collected some work just like this when I was younger. Our family is on a mailing list and there is an exhibition opening in Thessaloniki early next month. Jo, Anna, would you like to go to it?'

I pause because I don't know what will happen if we cannot find Teo but I do know Mama has asked me to try for us. Vasilios or a gallery that knows him just might be able to help and, if not, I'll know I tried.

Then from a different part of the world Anna follows my lead and together we slowly nod, *yes. Please.*

Peia

That first night, after our muted farewells, we continued to walk, up, up and up. Mama told me not to look back, but I do anyway. I see our moonlit cypress tree and it seems like a magnet, pulling our mothers down, down, down towards it. The priest walks with us for a little while to the top of our range. Then he quietly blesses us, hugs Agnete, whispers with Vaska and turns back. He is no longer our Pied Piper.

Vaska assumes the lead. Agnete walks behind him. Our mothers allocated locum parents to each child before we set off. The arrangements are working. Some of the older children are carrying the younger children, who, despite the early excitement of our adventure, are falling asleep on their backs and shoulders. At the back, we are three. I hold Adelphos's wounded hand in mine. He is not breaking ranks. Teo holds his other hand. We walk most of the night, until we reach a hut.

'Peia, wake up, the truck is here.' Is it afternoon already? Agnete is shaking me. 'We need to get the children up and ready to go,' she says. Many of the children are whimpering. It is the first time that they have heard or seen a truck. Two armed soldiers give us food: bread, cheese, figs, beans and berries, which we devour in no particular order. Adelphos cannot use his left hand but manages well enough with his right. I peel back the bandage covering his wound. It looks gruesome.

Teo gets the antiseptic from Vaska. Adelphos starts shaking

when he sees the little bottle. I can't have him screaming. I dig into my coat pocket. 'Adelphos, shut your eyes and hold out your right hand.' He scrunches his eyes shut and flattens his right hand into which I place a kangaroo and its joey. He opens his eyes and laughs. Teo joins him. 'Adelphos, these are my magic animals. They give me courage when I am frightened. I will loan them to you to help you to be as brave as a bear while we get your hand better. Can you look after my animals for a while?' He and Teo stare at the strange animals. While Adelphos is mesmerised, I apply some more antiseptic and a cleaner bandage. There is no shaking or wailing.

Vaska helps the older soldiers bundle our party into the tray of the truck and then sits in the cab with the other soldiers. The truck starts up and the small children put their hands over their ears. 'Where are we going?' I ask Agnete.

'Vaska thinks the truck is taking us to the bottom of the next mountains.'

'Vaska "thinks"?' I ask.

'He doesn't know the whole plan,' she replies.

'I thought the idea was to keep us off the roads so that we won't be a target for the planes.' She shrugs and doesn't reply. I ask another question, 'Will the other soldiers walk the next mountains with us?'

'I don't know,' she replies. 'Vaska knows the mountains well. I feel safe with him.'

'One armed boy and nineteen other children doesn't seem like a great plan or great odds to me,' I reply. The truck lurches loudly and some children are thrown across the tray. I try to keep them seated as the truck grinds over roads that aren't really roads. We could walk faster than this. Children are crying. Children are vomiting. I try to get them to shut their eyes. I wish I could shut mine. A front wheel gets stuck in a pothole. We're unloaded and after much revving, the driver reverses the truck out of the pothole. We're reloaded. Most of the hairpin bends require several attempts. We cross a river and eventually, we pull into an embankment. The end of the road section is declared for the day.

In the twilight, we huddle at the side of a track as Vaska and the soldiers do a lot of talking and pointing upwards. I can follow most of it. We must keep off any vehicle roads and stick to donkey and sheep tracks. The soldiers will try to get the vehicle going again and meet us tomorrow. Apparently, it's safer to walk tonight than to stay here.

An old farmer appears from somewhere, walking towards us with donkeys that are carrying food and water bags. The soldiers look up and move towards him. The smaller children rush towards the donkeys. The soldiers tell us that the farmer will walk with us tonight.

We set off as it begins to drizzle. The farmer leads with one donkey. Vaska and Agnete are next. I insert us behind them, as I want to know what they know. Behind us follows a string of people beads, interspersed with some donkey beads. It's very quiet. It's hard to imagine that these are the same children who threw themselves so boisterously into our recent Cyclops production at the church. As the light fades, my eyes begin to adjust and my other senses begin to awake. I can smell the spring flowers even if I can't see them and I can hear the forest for miles. Birds finishing their day. Owls beginning theirs. We stop for a short break and I hear some rustlings in nearby leaves.

Teo whispers loudly, 'I don't like this dark.'

Adelphos hands Teo the kangaroos and asks, 'What is wrong with this dark, Teo?'

Teo answers, 'The moon is staring at me.'

'Probably it just wants to get to know you,' I say.

Vaska shouts, 'Teo, be quiet.'

'You too, Adelphos,' adds Agnete. 'You both need to be quiet. Listen to Vaska.'

The farmer speaks. 'Let's put some of the smaller children on the donkeys. They can take turns through the night. The bigger children can lead the donkeys.' He shows us how to give a donkey an ear rub and receives a nuzzle in return. Teo and Adelphos are smitten and happily agree to become donkey leaders. Teo, donkey right. Adelphos, donkey left. A great distraction. The donkeys are loaded with some smaller-than-Teo-and-Adelphos-sized children, who are smiling for the first time since we set out.

We drop to the back. I don't think I'm going to learn anything more from the front at this stage. 'We can play a whisper game,' I say to the boys, 'It's called "When We Get There". I'll start. When we get there, I am going to adopt a bear. Now, the next person must say something that begins with a "C" and a "D".'

From a donkey, a quiet tired voice says, 'When we get there, I am going to cuddle a donkey.'

Teo whispers, 'When we get there, I am going to eat a forest. Adelphos?'

'When we get there, I am going to grow a new hand,' he whispers.

We play this game in the dark as we ascend the mountain. The small children rotate, taking turns on the donkeys. Towards dawn, our group reaches another hut. We stop and eat food from the donkey bags. The farmer stays as we settle down. He then speaks with Vaska before he turns and heads down the slope with his donkeys again. 'What's the plan?' I ask Vaska.

'Today, we will share watch shifts and sleep, and tonight we will move closer to the border.'

'By ourselves?' I ask.

After a pause, Vaska answers, 'Soldiers will arrive with a truck.'

Anna

What a week. I can't sleep but someone I really like is asleep next to me. I'm looking at Jimmi's animation, which is now much more personal. Jimmi has been deeply affected by the refugee stories. He, who originally saw the islands as a perpetual party, has now documented tourists, locals and refugees cheek by jowl. When his grandchildren ask, 'Where were you when …?' He will say, 'I was there.'

I hope this week might change the world. There. I have shown my hand. Awake after midnight, I have no journalistic independence. That picture that hit the world this week. The bright red T-shirt and shorts. The dark-haired toddler, washed up on a beach. The family hoping for a new life in Canada. Ani and Jimmi were nearby recording diasporic people on the move. Jimmi's animation now has a little character who is mostly a pompom hat, eyes and legs. The eyes get bigger and bigger as his story of the refugee crisis unfolds.

Initially, it struck him as obscene that life could continue on as usual on the islands. Summer. The tourist season. People swimming, lazing on lounges, boating. But some of the boats weren't for playing. They were for surviving. Or not. He ranted, 'How can people just step over washed-up lifejackets on the beach? How can they laugh and drink at beach bars while gazing out to sea? Why can't they see beyond the horizon?' The animated eyes under the pompom become wider and wider.

On one particularly ranty night, Sinead had just heard that her ma had found some photos of her da working for an aid organisation in Greece. He couldn't get work at home, so he came back.

Jimmi has started reading every book ever written and it's been hard for us to keep up with him. This week under the vines at our pub he said, 'The thing is, Civil Wars are the worst. There are no winners because humanity is at its basest. It is family against family and a generation is lost to them and the following generations are irrevocably changed by them. And then refugees become diasporic people and sometime after it will all happen again.'

Then he stopped ranting so much and his animation started to incorporate care, compassion, kindness, generosity and empathy.

Another picture hit me personally this week. Tonight, brought to us by the letter 'V'. A crowded gallery inside. People spilling onto the pavement outside. A huge 'V' in lights above it all.

'V' is also for Vancouver where Vasilios ventured. Where his mother recently died. Mum and Vasilios. Two people who hadn't seen each other for over three decades stood taking each other in. No words from either and neither filled the silence.

His work has no artist's statement. I like him already. His art speaks for itself. Abstract. But clear. Movement of legs, feet, arms, hands, heads as separate cubist shapes. Like Jimmi's, with the placement of the artist in the story. Vasilios has symbols of himself in his pieces. In some paintings, his hand is painting the picture or holding a sign pointing to land. His arms enfold people.

And then he was enfolding my mother and she was enfolding him. I did not hover. I watched them briefly from a distance, let myself feel happy for a moment and then went outside for a cigarette with Theo. I'm allowing myself to feel happy right now as well. It is after midnight and it is raining and Theo is next to me and sound asleep after a very long flight from Australia. Time to spoon.

Peia

Agnete asks, 'Vaska, would you like me to take first watch with you?'

'No, you settle the others and sleep first. Peia, will you watch with me?' Vaska asks.

I am surprised he has asked me. 'Yes,' I reply and we settle on some nearby rocks. He starts whittling.

'This helps me stay awake.' In between looking up and around, his deft hands work calmly on a small branch. 'I'm sorry I yelled at Teo. I'm tired.'

'We are all tired,' I respond. 'And there was no need for Agnete to join in. How far are we from the border?'

'Not too far but it's hard to work out the best route. The commander says it will be much easier if we can use the truck for part of it.'

'Is there any doubt about the truck?' I ask.

'I'm not sure they will be able to fix it,' he says. 'So it might not be here tonight?' I ask.

'That's right,' he says.

'Vaska, I'm not sure that going on the roads from here is a good idea. Surely the government troops will be keeping an eye on the roads near the border.'

'We haven't got much choice,' he says.

'We have. Stay off the roads. Walk on the tracks. We are all used to them. They are our advantage.'

'It will be much slower,' he says.

'It will be slower but safer. What's the great rush anyway?' I ask.

'I don't know,' he answers. 'My orders are to get through as soon as possible.'

'We have food and water and I'm sure farmers will help out with more,' I reply.

'I just hope the truck turns up,' he says.

Later in the day, I'm woken from my sleep in the hut by rats running over me. The boys make a game of chasing them outside but more sit up on the roof beams waiting to take their place. Agnete and Vaska are on watch. I walk towards them. There is no truck in sight, not even the rumble of one to be heard and no farmers are materialising in the mountain twilight.

Before I can even ask, Vaska answers my question, 'I think something must have happened to them or they would have got here somehow, or sent someone.'

'We should just lie low and wait. We can find a cave. We have food and water,' I reply.

'It's too quiet. I think we should move,' says Vaska.

'On the mountain tracks?' I ask. 'The road will be faster,' he says.

'It is more open. More dangerous,' I argue.

Agnete speaks, 'I agree with Vaska. Let's just get there.'

'Agnete, we don't even know where "there" is, other than up. We are children of the mountains. We can navigate goat and donkey tracks. We are good at that.'

Agnete replies, 'I trust Vaska.'

'Agnete,' I say, 'We all need to work out together what gives the group the best chance. If something has happened to our soldiers below, the original plan for us needs to change.'

'Peia, I don't know these tracks,' Vaska says. 'But a road is a road.'

I point towards the continuation of the track we came off

yesterday. 'Vaska, Agnete, we have spent all of our lives navigating tracks like these. Why would we make ourselves a group of sitting ducks by walking along the middle of a road?'

Vaska answers, 'Because my orders haven't changed. We have to get through as soon as possible and the road will be more direct. The truck will be able to find us on the road. Let's get moving.' Agnete nods. Vaska looks at me. 'Peia?'

'Vaska, we don't even know where we need to get *through* to.'

He points, 'I know that *through* is somewhere at the end of that road and I think we should move higher tonight.'

Agnete nods as Vaska speaks. I'm not going to win this one. I reply, 'I'll help Agnete organise the others.'

For several hours, we walk up, up and up, following the winding road. The group is very quiet and even the mountains are soundless tonight. The weather changes as we climb higher. The temperature is cooler and the sky is moonless. Suddenly, we feel a reverberation. The sky is changing. Far-off lightning. The boys move closer to me. Thunder rumbles. It sounds too fast and too close. Teo reaches into his pocket and brings out the kangaroos. He and Adelphos hold hands, a joey peeping out from between their fingers. As we turn at the next bend, we see a stationary truck with its lights on and some soldiers standing across the road. Not our truck. Not our soldiers. Our appearance is of no surprise to them. Next, we find ourselves in the back of a truck with the armed soldiers, who are not much older than head-down, gun-less Vaska, who is not much older than me. He sits jammed between the soldiers.

Most of the children whimper as they try to fall asleep. Agnete, who has been avoiding making eye contact with me, looks as though she could be sleeping. The truck climbs higher and higher. The thunder is a far-off rumble. The children on either side of me are exhausted. I hope they are dreaming of donkeys. I need to look asleep but stay awake. It's a game. When I get there I will abscond on a bird. No, I will capture a dray. Maybe I could escape on a ferry? There are no ferries in the mountains.

I need to think of something before we get there. But where is '*there*'? Is it up before we go down? Or up to stay up? What would Odysseus do? I haven't got ten years and a trained team. Vaska's blank eyes offer no clues. The truck groans. We could walk faster than this. Use the time to think.

Eventually we stop as does the noise of the truck.

Jo

It is morning, and Vasilios and I are sitting on the Thessaloniki seafront. The White Tower is to our left, the port is to our right and our coffees are front and centre. The chef has agreed to cook us a pizza for breakfast for old time's sake.

After the exhibition, we ate with a large group high up in the old town. After everyone dispersed, we walked and walked from up to down and talked and talked. Now, we are here. I have not been up all night since Anna was a baby. We started our peak-to-port walk by sitting under the walls of the city's ancient and eerie fortress. Vasilios thinks his father spent some time here during the Junta and wants to find out for certain. I told him about Mama's rembetika dancing and her father awaiting execution. Was it the same fortress?

Overnight, I have related the recent Mama story and the much longer saga called 'Growing Up with Peia'. It is the first time I have disclosed these stories so fully to anyone outside the family. My shoulders feel lighter. I also discovered that Vasilios had a similar upbringing and has spent an excess amount of his adult life wondering why our brief but happy teenage encounter so furiously fanned the winds in each of our mother's minds.

We order more coffee. Vasilios says, 'I don't know where home is anymore. After Mama died I needed to come back to join some of her dots that had become my blots. I remember this place as a child, Australia as a teenager and Canada as an adult.'

Our pizza arrives with our coffee. He continues, 'My mama was in many ways a wonderful mother. It must have been huge for her to go to Australia with me after Papa died, but soon after you and I ate pizza together, we were suddenly off to Canada and she would never talk about it.'

The chef comes out to check on everything and we thank him for improvising on the usual breakfast menu. I see Theo and Anna promenading towards us on the boardwalk like locals. They blend in with each other and the place. Not like that night in the hospital corridor when he was a burley form, trailing behind her. 'Mum, pizza for breakfast?' Anna asks.

'Have some,' I reply. 'There is plenty.' Theo and Anna eat some and order coffees. Vasilios starts to say something and then stops and shakes his head. 'Go on,' I say.

'No, let's enjoy now.'

Anna interjects quickly, 'I want to know anything that might help us with the mystery of Yiayia's life as a young girl.' I nod in agreement. As does Theo. Anna's phone rings. 'It's Sinead,' she says. 'Sorry, I'd better take it. It will be about meeting up.' She starts talking as the coffees arrive. 'Sinead, slow down, slow down, what photograph?' She sips some coffee, walks away, finishes the conversation and returns. 'She and Jimmi are catching a late afternoon ferry to the island tomorrow. She's sending me the details. Sorry, Vasilios, please continue.'

'The night my mama died she talked about walking in her northern mountains with younger children to another country,' Vasilios says. 'I thought it was all part of her dying mind wandering; however, she repeated the same story several times. Each time, she would get to the part about a lake, begin to cry and start all over again.' Anna's phone beeps, alerting us that she has received a text message.

Vasilios continues, 'I was waiting for Mama to say something like, "You are the best son in the whole world" but her last words to me were, "The mountains are in the box".' I know that feeling of expecting some loving affirming words and instead receiving a cryptic puzzle. 'In her small hand-carved box, made by my father, I found a note, "V, phone this number".' It was a Greek number.

Theo is first in, 'And did you?'

'No. I needed to make some art first.' Anna asks, 'Will you?'

'I think I can now. My exhibition is up and I don't feel so alone.'

Anna

We are on the graffiti express, a vibrant political protest on wheels. Across the aisle, before he fell asleep next to Theo, Vasilios's last slow words were, 'This is very special art, painting trains is speed work.' As we boarded he was texting on his phone. Theo is now jammed in by the window and Mum is enjoying her odyssey in what she is calling 'The Real Greece'. I remind her that she lives in it most days in Australia.

'No,' she replies to me. 'After hearing about Vasilios's life, I have decided that my corner in Australia is Celtic Greece.'

'Well,' I say, 'last night you got off to a good start in the real Greece by staying up all night.'

Mum laughs and says, 'And I am now being very Australian by sleeplessly heading to a party on the other side of the country. It was very sweet of Theo's mother to invite Vasilios too.'

'Yes, and to invite Sinead and Jimmi. That's the real Greece,' I say. 'Theo has been very quiet,' Mum observes.

'Yes, he is worried about the memorial service and carrying too much guilt. He did everything he could.'

Her eyes are a strange mix of very alive and very tired. 'Yes, he has fused guilt and grief. However, he told me on the plane that he is very pleased that we are going with him.'

'I am very pleased we are going with him too.' I take her hand in mine.

'We haven't needed an apology since I arrived,' Mum says.

'Mum, just before we got on the train, Sinead sent me a photograph of her daideó. I keep looking at it, closing it and looking at it again. I think you should see it.'

She nods and I click on the black-and-white image of a young male aid worker standing with a group of what looks like refugee children and teenagers. Sinead says the photo is dated 1948. Mum holds the photograph close to her eyes, then at a distance, before bringing it in again.

'Mum at one stage you said that Yiayia had sleep-talked about "mountains", "children" and "walking". Sinead doesn't know the full details yet but she thinks the photo might be in one of the camps in the north of Greece that took in the Greek children crossing the borders during the Civil War. I know it's a long shot but records from those camps might just help us find Teo. I still don't know what happens if we can't find him.'

'Anna, I don't know what happens if we don't find him but we are giving it our best shot. In all my life I haven't felt this close to my adopted mama. That's huge for me and I think it might be for her too. She asked me to find Teo for "us" and she has never been a great one at asking me or you or anyone for assistance.'

All our fellow travellers are asleep as the train clunkity, clunkity, clunks its way south. Mum continues, 'Whether we find Teo or not, I'm worried about what and who we'll find on the way, like Vasilios, and how I will be able to tell her about finding him, without it seeming like a deliberate distraction or a huge betrayal of whatever she was perhaps trying to protect me from back then.'

I say, 'I think Dado gave those canvases to you for a reason.' My head rests comfortably on her shoulders. Painting trains might be speed work but this train is not speedy.

Peia

It is sunrise when we are butted out of the trucks with a force disproportionate to our size. The boys cling closely together. Vaska stays in the truck with some soldiers. We walk in a line with soldiers in front and behind us. The nearby pines are fragrant. The granite peaks above us are raw. Falcons circle above us. We walk down until we reach some huts. It's like an amphitheatre with a beautiful mountain lake as the stage. I imagine a ferry on it. There are birds, ducks, geese and storks.

After days of donkey rations, we are welcomed to the hut by women who present us with a feast. I haven't seen such food since Teo's party all those years ago. Cheese, tzatziki, greens, sausage, dolmas, beans and zucchini. As we line up to be served, I say to Agnete, 'That was a great plan of yours to use the road. It was certainly a short way to get to a quick meal.'

She replies, 'You agreed to the plan too and if this is how the enemy eats then we are on the wrong side.'

I look her straight in the eye. 'This food would have been forcibly taken. It is a trap to lure us in.'

'Well, it's working. Look at the children eating,' she replies. 'Our side has abandoned us. The truck never came back and we never even received a message. They just wanted to sign the women up and get us away from the bombing so it wouldn't be on their conscience.'

I don't want to hear such things. I raise my voice, 'Agnete, I don't know what happened. But Mama and Papa would never abandon me and I won't abandon them. You are like Polyphemus, the Cyclops, blinded and fooled.'

She storms off. I sit down to eat with Teo and Adelphos because I need to talk to them.

Anna

Odysseus would be proud of our multimodal meanderings. It's early evening and we are on foot, transferring from the train to the bus. The city is quietly getting on with its post-siesta and pre-night business. Vasilios, who is texting while walking, lags behind us. Older people shouldn't do that; text and walk. It makes them dangerous and slow. He calls out that he'll catch up to us. Mum says that she will wait for him. The bus station is in sight and we need to grab something to eat before our night ride to the west coast. 'What's next?' asks Theo.

'Food and drink?' I answer.

'No,' he replies, 'I mean the big "next". *Megalo* next.'

'Bigger than the memorial service and your mother's party?' I ask.

'Yes. Bigger than them.'

'Bigger than finding Teo?'

'Yes. Bigger even than finding Teo.'

'Is "*us next*" bigger than all that?'

'I think it is, don't you?' he asks.

'Theo there is something about you and your timing of questions about "us" when I am in transit.'

'So, you don't think "*us next*" is bigger than all that?'

'Theo, I really like you and it's great that you are here and that we are together here.' We've now reached the terminal where huge buses are heading in from all over. 'But I'm just not sure what your version of "*us next*" involves. Let's grab that table up there. Does your "*us next*" involve me dropping everything here and heading back to Australia with you?'

I head to the table, park my case and look back. As he hoists his suitcase up a step, a wheel comes off. 'Bugger,' he says loudly as the wheel heads down a gutter onto the road and under a parked bus. And then, there I am, not under the bus, but next to him, giving him a hug. I'd like it to be one of our more complicated hugs but this will have to do for the moment. I take one of his hands, and he picks up his suitcase in the other. We head to our table.

'Theo, I'm a bit of a one-step-at-a-time girl. Next, could we just eat, drink and catch the bus?' A solemn nod. 'And could I sit next to you on the bus?' A cheeky nod. His phone beeps.

'Look at these. Impressive.' He beams as he shows me some photographs displaying the deconstruction and reconstruction of the shed. Progress. 'She has done it so quickly. It's going to be stunning.' As long as she is not stunning. Mum and Vasilios see us and wave. Theo runs to show Mum the photographs. 'Any other news?' I ask as we all sit.

'Yes,' says Vasilios, 'Just a bit. The Greek number has responded to my text. He will meet us at our ferry terminal in the morning. He lives on Ithaca.'

Peia

The boys and I enjoy a long talk and a slow feast, after which I rebandage Adelphos's hand, which is oozing. As I bind his hand, I see Agnete chatting with a soldier at the door. I listen to the children as they run around the lake and try to imagine that I am in a dense magical forest. Suddenly, Agnete appears at my side. I say, 'They are restless, let's do a play. They liked "Odysseus and the Cyclops". You narrate, I'll call the children together.'

When I have rounded up the cast, she asks, 'Who would like to be Odysseus?' The child with the tired voice from the donkey volunteers. 'What about Odysseus's crew?' she asks. Teo, Adelphos and others volunteer. She has the cast, so she starts, 'Odysseus and his crew were sailing home from Troy.' The team is rowing. Better than last time. My head is stretched up on alert. I can't let it disappear into my neck. This is no place for a Quitter Bird.

Some soldiers watch the play from their barracks as do the women clearing up the food. All is going well, both the cast and the audience are engaged. As we reach the bit where Odysseus, after so many of his crew have been eaten, is thinking of a plan, I feel a tap on my shoulder and a muzzle in my back. A voice speaks, 'This way, Miss.'

I see Teo and Adelphos watching me. I head with the soldier towards the barracks where Vaska is sitting on the steps chatting with some soldiers. He looks up and walks towards me. I can still hear the play; the giant is asking Odysseus his name. I hear Odysseus reply, 'My Name is Nobody.'

Vaska makes no eye contact with me but says to the soldier, 'She's the one.'

I cry out, 'Which one?'

I hear a blind giant waking his neighbours, who call to him, asking, 'Who has done this to you?'

Vaska looks away and I grab his face and scream, 'Which one am I?' The soldier roughly pulls me back and another one joins him. I shriek at Vaska again, 'Which one am I?' I can see the players and the women looking this way. The play has moved.

Vaska says, 'She will never pledge allegiance to the King and Queen.'

I scream, 'Yes, my name is Peia and I am not blinded and fooled by the King and Queen.'

Agnete is now standing next to Vaska and yelling, 'She is too stubborn to sign.'

The soldier pushes the gun into my back and says, 'Everyone has a price.'

Stork, stand steady. Keep the drama here. I shriek, 'Agnete, what was your price? Protecting your father? Saving Vaska?'

She opens her mouth, as a voice from downslope calls out, 'Can we finish the play?'

Agnete calls back, 'We will finish it tomorrow. Go to bed now.'

The gun is pushing harder into my back as I continue, 'What was your lie, Agnete? What was your lie, Vaska?' He looks at his feet.

Agnete speaks to the gathered soldiers, 'My father told me that her father is a traitor and that her mother slavishly follows his commands.'

I reply, 'And what about your father, our priest?'

She slaps my face hard and says, 'My father had to do what was best for the village.'

As he drags me away, the soldier says, 'Let's see what your price is.'

Jo

The port is gearing up for the day. An old man and Vasilios hug. It is a still, silent hug. I would be twitching by now, but these two seem to know that this is exactly what they should do. Anna, Theo and I are here but we are not here. We are a little away to the side in the wings, waiting for a cue, if one comes.

In between sips of coffee, Anna and Theo are stretching their limbs like professional athletes. The old man is not a little old man. He has to bend down to hug the not-so-short Vasilios. The man's neatly trimmed grey beard defines a triangle-shaped face with black arched eyebrows that line up nicely with his black moustache. If they do not move soon, they will be mistaken for a life statue and people will start dropping coins near them. I am not good at slow but if I move I might miss something. At last they start talking to each other and Vasilios beckons to me. On cue, I move and Vasilios introduces me. 'Jo, this is Kyrios Kouris.' The man says, 'Please call me Adelphos.'

The man shakes my hand. 'Pleased to meet you,' he says. We walk towards Theo and Anna. She will be beside herself at having had to wait so long. Not her usual style. The old man greets them and says, 'We are all travelling on the same ferry this morning. I'm heading home.' A boarding announcement booms out as he asks, 'Shall we get some seats together?'

The locals rush to board as though their lives depend on it. We move in the crush led by an agile Adelphos, who goes ahead with his light backpack while we park our bags in the luggage bays as directed. He beckons to us from a window near a roomy seat bay with a table in the middle. When we reach him, he explains that ticketed seat numbers don't matter all that much. Coffees appear for all of us.

As the ferry reverses, Vasilios talks slowly, 'Adelphos was one of the younger children who was on that walk with my mama to another country.' If there was a group photograph now, it would show our faces, eyes agog and our hands clutching small paper coffee cups. He continues, 'I think Mama was reliving the walk as she died.' He begins to choke up. I take a hand. Adelphos asks Vasilios if he would like him to speak. Vasilios nods slowly.

'It was only about two years ago that I found Vasilios's mother.' We listen. Today, a sea the colour of the bluest Greek postcard is our backdrop. 'She had hidden herself very well overseas. We northern mountain children are very good at hiding.'

Anna's and Theo's faces express total concentration. Anna asks, 'Why did you contact her after so long?'

He pauses before answering, 'It took me many, many decades to want to find some missing pieces of my life. During the Greek Civil War our village was being bombed. Most of the men were away fighting. The women kept us fed and safe.' Nearby, a group has cracked open a deck of cards. 'A decision was made that groups of children would walk to safe countries to the north. We would be accompanied by soldiers from our democratic army and older village girls. Vasilios's mother was one of those girls.'

Anna asks, 'You were one of the Greek children that crossed Greece's northern borders?'

'Not quite but I got close.' A young man comes over and hugs Adelphos, who turns to us and says, 'I'm so sorry. I did not know my grandson would be on the ferry. I need to talk to him.'

Story interruptus. How did this happen? He is ours. No wonder so many Greek epics go on for years. Smokers are enjoying the bow. Theo's, Anna's and Vasilios's eyes are fixed there too. 'You two catch up,' I say to Adelphos. 'We'll get a little fresh air.'

The four of us stand outside, silently inhaling. Then Vasilios speaks, 'I do and I do not want to hear more about Mama's journey.'

Theo says, 'She must have been very brave. They all must have been very brave.'

Anna is thinking out loud. 'After her stroke, Yiayia sleep-talked of "mountains", "children" and "walking" but she must have got north of the border to get to Australia?'

Two young boys are running around near us enjoying their freedom. I see that the young man and Adelphos are engaged in deep conversation. Anna sees them too and says, 'I don't think we are going to learn any more on this ferry trip.'

Theo speaks again, 'I wonder if Adelphos would like to come to my mother's birthday party tonight?'

We finish our cigarettes. A need for sleep overwhelms me. We settle in some seats and the next thing I am aware of is an announcement, telling us that we are approaching Vathy, our next and final port. Anna is standing on the bow next to Theo who is clinging on to it like a figurehead. Breathing in home?

Anna

Theo's family also holds multi-event parties. It's his mother's sixtieth and name day. It's also a party for his yiayia's eightieth. Additionally, it's a welcome party for the extended Australian, Canadian, Irish and Swedish connections and a welcome home party for Theo. His mother, Hermioni, and his Yiayia Rosalia haven't stopped smiling since they saw him. I bet they hope that he will stay. It's also a reunion between Mum and Hermioni and a sort of reunion between Hermioni and Vasilios. He can't remember having met her but she can remember his pivotal role in the seventies pizza saga.

Theo and I are sitting outside on either side of his Yiayia Rosalia on the stage of a stunning natural amphitheatre. I would love it if my yiayia were here with us. Behind us, a terraced hill leads up to the house. In front of us, there is a dramatic pink sunset over the sea.

Earlier this evening, we went to church for the memorial service. Theo found it calming. 'Yiayia, I was worried that I might leave the service even sadder but I feel lighter. How does that work?'

She holds his hands tightly and speaks, 'There is something about being with others and sharing deep grief. All those years ago, when I encouraged your mother to stay in Australia after your pappoú died, I thought I could cheat grief by just miming the rituals. It didn't work.' From the house, soft music and singing drifts our way. Definitely not rembetika. No weeping and wailing. It is guitar not bouzouki. Much lighter. More gentle. Yiayia Rosalia continues, 'I came crashing down and your mama and papa came running home with you and stayed. I didn't mean that to happen but you all helped bring me back to life.'

Sinead walks outside. We beckon her down and she joins us. 'I'm hiding from Jimmi who wants to teach me Ithacan dancing. Talk about a little knowledge being a dangerous thing. After what you said about Vasilios's art, I suggested he show Vasilios his animation. They are now best friends.'

Rosalia takes both Sinead's hands, examines them and asks, 'Have you lost someone? Are you on a search?'

I look at Theo. He is all eyes.

'Yes,' answers Sinead. 'How do you know?'

Theo raises one of his bullshit meter eyebrows and says, 'Yiayia? Now? Outsiders?'

So we are outsiders, Theo? Yiayia Rosalia answers my question. 'Theo, they are hardly outsiders and if I can assist I will.' Theo looks very bashful and while palmistry isn't taught as a fundamental in journalism schools, you just never know from where good information might come. The smell of the food follows the sound of the music down the hill. I show Rosalia the phone picture of Sinead's grandfather. Sinead says, 'That's the man whose story I am searching for. He is my grandfather. I've been researching his time in Greece. I think the photo might be in one of the camps in the north of Greece that took in the Greek children crossing the borders during the Civil War.'

Yiayia Rosalia says, 'That photo could be in one of those camps.'

Theo's mother, Hermioni is walking towards us, carrying a tray of food and some wine. She calls out, 'May I sit with you?' We all nod. She places the food and wine on the table. Theo pulls up a chair for her as she serves us from a big bowl of pasta. She says, 'Don't let me stop the conversation.'

Theo pours some wine and Rosalia asks, rhetorically, I think, 'Hermioni, you have told Theo that I was once in prison?'

'Not yet,' Hermioni answers.

Rosalia replies, 'Well, yet can be now. It was after the Greek Civil War when many of us refused to sign allegiance to the monarchy. I was imprisoned on the other side of Greece for three years on an island with women.'

Peia

The stork is curled compactly in the cell corner and is becoming smaller and smaller as the punching gets harder and harder. She is then left alone, just long enough for her head to emerge from her neck before she is struck again. She coils herself up while she is alone. She feels numb for a little while. Then she feels a wall of cold water and a series of mighty kicks to her stomach and jarring along her back. More icy water. More shudders. More determination. Every part of her is flexed. She will not sign.

Sometime before dawn she hears, 'Maybe her price is watching us work on her brother?' She knows she needs to soar even though her head wants to disappear into her neck. She doesn't want the boys to be missed just yet. She tells the guard that she will sign the allegiance to the monarchy even though she has no intention of doing so.

It is after dawn before the boys are missed. Most of the soldiers go to the forest to search for them. A radio signal is coming through in the office. 'Can I use the toilet please?' she asks. A guard butts her into the toilet and heads towards the signal. She needs to soar above her pain and find the boys. As the guard talks on the radio, the winds move her towards life. She squeezes her bruised body out of the window and heads up to the forest away from the search party. Her sore shattered self somehow produces winged feet, which carry her to a cave where she sleeps.

The first night she was too sore to walk. Sleep and pain

overwhelmed her. Then there was a blur of nights and days. From her cave, each night she looked down at the campfires below and hoped that the boys were on the other side, above the lake.

She likes to imagine that she flew out of the cave with her graceful, long, broad black-and-white wings extended, her elegant unlined neck stretched forward and her slim red catwalk legs trailing. All in unison. Just like in the dance. She prefers this image to the start-stop reality of her black-and-red legs, full of pain and the feeling that her middle would never be the same again. It never was.

Anna

Mum arrived bearing a lit cigarette and a mint tin ashtray and we have moved to the side together.

Adelphos appears up near the house and Yiayia Rosalia is beckoning him.

'Mum, we can't let him get hijacked again,' I say.

'Anna, when in Greece …'

I move towards Rosalia as she gently takes Adelphos's hands in hers. 'Deep wound here,' she says. Mum sits with us.

'I hardly feel it anymore,' he replies.

'You can't fool me,' she says. 'Just because it has been there a long time, doesn't mean you don't feel it. It's from your childhood?' she asks.

'Yes, from when I had courage but not competence.'

'That sounds like the right combination for childhood,' she replies. She massages his left hand while he sits meditatively. This is too slow. Theo takes my hands and mirrors his yiayia's actions. I mutter something about outsiders.

Rosalia asks Adelphos, 'Have you always lived in Ithaca?'

'It took me years to find Ithaca,' he answers.

'Me too,' she says. 'Ithaca is my son-in-law's home.'

He replies, 'My childhood home was in the northern mountains where I hurt my hand.' Gentle guitar music plays in the background, as Jimmi's booming voice announces from the house that Ithaca is his soul's home.

'How did you hurt your hand?' she asks.

'I was one of the young children in the Greek Civil War who tried to walk out of Greece and I hurt my hand on a fence I was jumping. Vasilious's mother, Agnete, was an older girl who walked with us.'

'Did you make it out?' she asks.

'Not quite. Another girl, who was like a sister to me, became separated from us so her brother and I left the group. We didn't want to go on without her.'

Vasilios is standing next to Mum.

I ask, 'What were your friends' names?' He looks at me as Mum does. It's one of her looks. I may have overstepped a line here. He pauses. 'The girl was called Peia and the boy, my best friend, was called Teo. Adelphos and Teo. Teo and Adelphos.'

Mum has turned white.

He continues, 'Peia devised a plan to save the three of us after we had been caught by the army.'

Me again, 'What was the plan?'

'Peia guessed that she would be interrogated by the soldiers. So, she made that a decoy during a play narrated for us by Agnete, Vasilios's mother.' Vasilios, Mum and I look at each other.

'As she planned, we ran away shortly after she was led away. She was meant to join us three days later in the mountains.'

I'm digging in my handbag and then hand him the kangaroos. He is frozen.

'Peia's kangaroos. We left these in a cave for her to find. On top of a bed of acorns.'

I say, 'Peia is my yiayia.'

Mum adds, 'And my mother.'

There are no words, just soft music coming from the house.

Adelphos stands up, looks at all of us, then faces the sea and cries out, 'I turned to you when I turned my back on the mountains when they turned their back on me. You knew what happened and you never told me!' He turns back to us. 'Peia survived? Found the kangaroos?'

Mum and I nod. Adelphos is crying and hugging us. 'Peia, Peia, Peia. Her daughter. Her granddaughter.'

Between us and the house, the amphitheatre's lower slope is filling with a chorus coming down.

Vasilios slowly asks, 'Peia, Teo and you left my mother behind?'

Adelphos answers, 'Peia and Agnete had a falling out as teenage girls do.'

I ask, 'Where is Teo now?'

'The first night we found a cave high up and foraged nearby at a farm. We knew it was dangerous but Peia had said that she would join us in three days. When she didn't, we waited longer but were worried about being caught. And my hand was getting worse and Teo had become very sleepy.'

Sinead asks, 'What was wrong with Teo?'

'I didn't know but I knew we had to move,' Adelphos replies. 'We set out at night and went to the farm to gather some food but when we entered the barn, a farmer was waiting with a gun. "Just boys," he called out as he prodded us into his house. His wife took one look at us and prodded us outside with a scrubbing brush which she used on us in a tub of water.'

Theo asks, 'Which side were they on?'

'The side that was worried about my oozing hand and Teo's red spots and temperature.'

Vasilios asks, 'Where was my mother all this time?'

Adelphos lowers his head. 'We only spoke once on the phone when she was dying and that was one of the questions I asked her. She stayed with the rest of the group.' Vasilios kneels by him and holds his hand. Jimmi offers him a beer, which he accepts with his other hand. 'In our phone call, I found out that after the war your mother, Agnete, had been placed in a *Paidopoleis*, one of the Queen's children's homes. Her family was killed in an onslaught of village bombing soon after we left. Your father, Vaska, who was one of the soldiers who accompanied us, survived the war in gaol.' He pauses for a drink. 'However, he subsequently had many incarcerations, including one during the Junta when he died. After that, Agnete went with you to Australia. She told me that she and Vaska had never forgiven themselves for signing the allegiance to the King and Queen.'

Vasilios asks quietly, 'Why did they then?'

'She told me it was to save the lives of the group.' I ask, 'What happened to you and Teo?'

'On the farm, we had sanctuary, rest, food and care. My hand started to heal, but Teo's spots and high temperature were joined by coughing, nausea and vomiting. If nurture, nursing and love could have kept Teo alive, he would have lived. But he died in the arms of the farmer. Typhus.'

Sinead asks, 'How did you survive?'

'After we buried Teo on the farm, I lived there until I was reunited with my mother, Trenna, well after the war. My father died in the war and Mama knew that Peia's mother had died, fighting in one of the last big battles, and that her father had been executed in prison.'

Jimmi speaks quietly, 'There are no winners.' Sinead continues, 'Family against family.'

I hug Mum and say, 'A generation is lost to them and the generations that follow are changed by them.'

Jo

Anna, Adelphos and I talked and cried with Mama and Da in the morning after the party.

It was a spring evening in Australia. Mama and Da were sitting in front of the emerging shed, which is still a little bitsy but, even at a distance, I could see how all its incomplete but distinctive parts just might come together to form a unique and beautiful whole.

Adelphos told Mama that his son and grandson are named after Teo.

Mama is open to his offer to go north to try to find Teo's grave and he has invited Anna, Vasilios, Theo and me to join him and his sons on the trip if we wish.

When Mama heard what we had discovered, she just nodded slowly. However, at the end of the Skype she said, 'For us. For us.'

Da has since reported that she is improving every day. I am going to stay on for a few months, rent a studio and make some art.

Theo was very moved by hearing about his yiayia's imprisonment. He's going back to Australia for a while, as he told his boss he would return, but he is planning to come back to Greece to study architecture for, as he says, 'Where else would you study architecture?'

Ani wants Anna, Sinead and Jimmi to stay on, keep covering the financial crisis and join more dots in their stories to make a documentary. Anna likes the title 'A Shed Called Ithaca'; however, I imagine that there will be a few more beers in that Irish pub before a title, let alone the content, is decided.

Glossary

ANZAC: Australian and New Zealand Army Corps (1914–18).
Apaisiodoxía: Pessimism.
Banshee: An Irish female spirit whose wailing warns of death.
Craic: Enjoyable conversation.
Da: Father.
Daddo: Grandfather.
Daideó: Grandfather.
Dolmades: Stuffed vine leaves.
Dolmas: Stuffed vegetables.
Esy: You.
Fasolada: Dry white bean soup.
Filo: Very thin unleavened dough.
Galaktoboureko: Creamy, custard dessert made with filo pastry.
Glödkaka: Cheers.
Haima: Blood.
Hatchet: Brilliant.
Hronia Pola: Happy Birthday.
Iskhein: Keeping back.
Kalimera: Good morning.
Kalispera: Good evening. (Also used in the afternoon)
Kolokithokeftedes: Zucchini fritters.
Leípei: Missing.
Lypiménos: Sad.
Megalo: Large.

Melancholikós: Depressed.
Mórai: Grandma.
Mou: Me.
Paidopoleis: Children's homes established by the Greek Queen.
Papa: Father.
Pappoú: Grandfather.
Plaka: A popular neighbourhood in Athens.
Rembetika: The music of Greece's impoverished and dispossessed.
Saganaki: A dish prepared in a small frying pan.
Shebang: The whole of something.
Sigà, sigà: Slowly, slowly.
Sláinte: Good health.
Souvlaki: Pieces of grilled meat on a skewer.
Spanakopita: Spinach with cheese and herbs in filo pastry.
Sygnómi: Sorry.
Tha mou leípeis: You will be missing from me.
Tha mou leípsoun: They will be missing from me.
Theía: Aunt.
Theío: Uncle.
Tiropitakia: Filo pastry feta cheese triangles.
Tzatziki: Yoghurt, garlic and cucumber dip.
Yamas: Cheers.
Yassou: Hello.
Yiayia: Grandmother.

Acknowledgements

Finding Teo is a fictional work created towards my 2020 Master of Applied Arts and Humanities (Research) at the University of Canberra, Australia. Many generous staff assisted in the novel's development. In particular: Dr. Tony Eaton who smoothed many paths; Felicity Packard, whose enthusiasm as my initial advisor fueled my enthusiasm; Dr. Jennifer Crawford, for her oversight and insight; and Distinguished Professor Jen Webb, especially for her support of my navigation through voice, culture and representation.

For the inspiration, my heartfelt gratitude goes to Chloe (not her real name). *Finding Teo* is not her story, but there would be no *Finding Teo* if not for our discussions in Greece, where she shared some of her experience of the Greek Civil War, including that she was one of the 24,000 Greek children evacuated and that Australia had joined international efforts to reunite children with their families.

For superb editing assistance throughout four years of novel (and thesis) writing, my love and thanks go to ninety-nine year old Diana Hall for her long haul with me. For more recent editing assistance, thanks to Susan Hall and, for design and photography, Robin Hall.

For support during writing in Europe thanks to: Hazel for guiding me in the mountains of South-West Bulgaria; Vasiliki Kartsiakli and Basil Nanis, archaeologists and Thessaloniki locals, for background literature and an insightful and poignant exploration of the Greek Civil War on foot; and Evelyn Callaghan, for providing an Emerald Isle haven, where I immersed creatively with my Irish forebears and found some of their imagined descendants a home in *Finding Teo.*

For manuscript enrichments, thanks to: Petro Georgiou, for sharing from his extensive experience and considered perspective; Jenna Daroczy, particularly around tricenarians and journalism; Meaghan Rennison, around strokes and occupational therapy; and Bianca Tzatzagos, for direction and correction around Greek language and culture.

Thanks to family and friends who had faith in me, showed interest and tolerated my absences. Very belated appreciation (which in all likelihood was not expressed at the time) to teachers who inspired my love of Greek history, drama, myths and legends. And, to a master-of-the-tale, Brian Hungerford, who years ago told me a story (that has lingered) about why he gave up the day job and pursued his love of storytelling.

Permissions

Every effort has been made to contact the copyright holders of material produced in this text. In cases where these efforts were unsuccessful the copyright holders are asked to contact the publisher directly.

Lyrics excerpt from *Midnight Rain*, Paul Kelly, 2001, is reproduced with permission of Sony Music, Australia. Lyrics excerpt from *Coat of Arms*, 2010, is reproduced with kind permission of Sabaton. Lyrics from *Night Descended Without Moon*, Apostolos Kaldaras, 1947, are reproduced with kind permission of his estate.

Some lines from *Ithaka*, C.P. Cavafy, 1911, are used with great reverence for their perpetual relevance. Some references to being six come from *The End*, A. A. Milne, 1927. Some lyrics from *Galway Bay*, Arthur Colahan, 1947, are used with veneration for their timeless evocation, as are some lyrics from *Never on Sunday*, Manos Hatzidakis, 1960. Irish poet, William Butler Yeats is widely attributed for 'there are no strangers here, only friends you haven't met yet' which appears in Irish pubs and other interesting places throughout the world.

Marjorie Morrissey

Born and bred in Canberra, Marjorie started her career as a teacher in NSW and subsequently worked overseas and elsewhere in Australia. In 1996, she started a love affair with Australia's Northern Territory where she lived and had an executive career for many years. More recently, she returned to home base from where she was lucky enough to have more time for travel (when possible), study and writing. *Finding Teo* was conceived overseas, is her first novel and was written as part of her 2020 Master of Applied Arts and Humanities (Research).

CPSIA information can be obtained
at www.ICGtesting.com
Printed in the USA
BVHW070119161221
624018BV00010B/1540